ONE IN FIVE

A SELENA BAILEY NOVELLA

H.K. CHRISTIE

KEEKSTAR
MEDIA

ALSO BY H.K. CHRISTIE

The Selena Bailey Novella Series

Not Like Her, Book 1 is the first novella in the suspenseful Selena Bailey Novella series. If you like thrilling twists, dark tension, and smart and driven women, then you'll love this series.

One In Five, Book 2

On The Rise, Book 3

The Unbreakable Series

The Unbreakable Series is a heart-warming women's fiction series, inspired by true events. If you like journeys of self-discovery, wounded heroines, and laugh-or-cry moments, you'll love the Unbreakable series.

We Can't Be Broken, Book 0

Where I'm Supposed To Be, Book 1

Change of Plans, Book 2

Copyright © 2019 by H.K. Christie

Cover design by Suzana Stankovic

www.authorhkchristie.com

First edition: December 2019

ISBN -13: 978-0-9982856-4-1

For Emily Paige

1

he End. At last, Selena was finished writing the umpteenth paper for her freshman English class. The assignment was to write an essay about a life-changing experience. She'd been concerned that if she wrote her real story her professor would be horrified, so she'd taken a bit of a creative license by attributing her mother's death to a lost battle with cancer instead of the more accurate account of her mother's long illness with alcohol followed by being murdered by her scumbag boyfriend. *Details.* Either way, it had been profound. It led Selena into the arms of her very own deranged psychopath and eventually to a reunion with her father. She'd omitted the deranged psycho boyfriend bit. That would be for her next essay —she was running out of topics for the class and she still had two months left before the winter break.

The sound of a key turning in the lock caused her body to react. She sat up, grabbed for her baton from under her pillow, and prepared herself for an attack. It was more than likely just her roommate, but she had been in self-defense and weapons training with her stepmother, Martina, for the last nine months. Martina had drilled into her that, as a smaller female, she'd have to always be prepared for a potential threat. Martina insisted that at her size, weapons and being on high alert would be her only saving grace if she were to be assaulted. Initially, Selena had taken offense at the smaller female remark. At five foot three inches, she wasn't too vertically challenged—but considering she could still shop in the kids section, she'd promised to be vigilant.

The door opened and in strolled her roommate, Dee Hankel, a Chemistry major and fellow freshman at San Francisco University, who Selena was sure was never referred to as a small female and likely hadn't shopped for children's clothing since she was, well, a child. Dee was her polar opposite. A tall, blond ex-volleyball player that spent as much time partying as she did studying. Dee was a work hard, play hard type. Selena was a work hard type—end of sentence. She relaxed her body and stuffed her weapon back under her pillow. "Hey, Dee."

Dee slurred a, "S'up, girl. You studying?"

Considering it was Saturday at eleven, it wasn't shocking Dee had already hit her first party of the night. Selena nodded. "Yep. More essays. Super fun."

"You need to get out more. C'mon, there's a party down the hall. That totes cutie who was eyeing you is there. Whass'ss name. Brandon? Brando? Brendon? Whatever. He asked about you."

Heat filled her cheeks. "Pass." Not that *Brendon* wasn't cute or smart, she just wasn't going to go there. She was officially off men for, *um, let me think, oh right, life.* Considering her last boyfriend, the deranged psychopath, kidnapped her and then tried to shoot her in the head, a break from men was definitely in order. Even if he was cute. *No need to kidnap and torture this gal twice. Lesson learned.*

Dee stumbled onto the bed across from Selena's and laid on her stomach, with her head on her pillow. She turned toward

Selena. "Oh, c'mon. It's just down the hall. You need to have some fun. All work and no play is *no bueno*. You'll burn out and jump off the top floor. Seriously, girl. I worry about you. College is about fun and new experiences!" She rolled off the bed and then kneeled down in front of Selena. "Please! Pretty please! Come out with me!"

Selena was sure she'd had all the coed fun she'd ever need, but she supposed she could use a break. "Fine. I'll go. Give me a sec to change."

Dee popped up and clapped her hands enthusiastically. "Yeah! Selena's getting her groove back!"

Selena slid off the bed and headed to the dresser. She pulled out a pair of black skinny jeans and a white cable-knit sweater with a plaid scarf for warmth as well as a splash of color. She wasn't sure there was a groove to get back, but she'd at least look presentable. She slipped on the new digs and made her way to the bathroom to brush out her hair. In front of the mirror she undid the messy bun and brushed her long chestnut locks before applying a red shimmery lip gloss and adding mascara to her long lashes.

She returned to the common area where Dee was furiously texting on her phone. Selena said, "I'm ready."

Dee glanced up. "Damn. You clean up. You look like a Disney princess—that one that has a friend who was a genie ... you know the one."

Dee was blitzed. Selena shook her head. "You mean Jasmine?" It wasn't the first time someone had made the correlation.

Dee's aqua blue eyes went wide. "Yes! That's it! You should dress up as Jasmine for Halloween!"

Selena didn't dress up for Halloween, and she certainly didn't dress up as a scantily clad princess. "Let's not get carried away. You ready?"

"Oh, come on! Halloween is next week, I heard the parties are epic."

Hand on hip, Selena asked, "You ready?"

"Yes, Jeez. Let's go."

As Selena followed Dee out the door and down the hall, Selena had a feeling she would be regretting this decision. The sounds of Bruno Mars's latest hit could be heard as soon as they stepped out of their room. They strolled until Dee stopped in front of the first open door, which was obviously the source of the blaring music. She said, "You ready for some fun?"

"Sure."

Dee giggled and grabbed Selena's hand, dragging her inside the dorm room. Selena assessed the party. There were about twenty people with red Solo cups in hand in a space that comfortably held about half of that. Before Selena could react, someone shoved a cup in her hand. She sniffed the cheap beer and glanced up. Her eyes locked with Brendon's big brown eyes. A fellow freshman, originally from the central valley, majoring in Political Science. Medium height. Medium cute. *One hundred percent not interested*. She handed the cup back to him. "I don't drink."

His face fell. "Oh, sorry. Seriously? I didn't know." He took it back.

His sincerity almost made her feel sorry for him. "It's fine. I just don't like it." *Like, I don't like the idea of becoming an alcoholic like my deceased mother.*

"Oh, okay. Um. How are you?"

Selena gave him the side eye. "I'm good. You?" This was going to be painful. She should just go back to her dorm room.

"I'm alright. I just finished my midterm for English. Ugh, if I have to write one more paper, I'm not sure what I'll do."

Selena cracked a grin. "I hear you. I just finished mine too.

I'm so tired of essays. I want to get into my major classes, you know?"

He ran his hand over his floppy brown hair. "Criminal Justice, right?"

He remembered. *Poor guy, he does have a crush.* "Yep."

"What do you want to do with your degree?"

That is a good question. "I'm not sure. Maybe become a police officer or investigator or something. Right now, I work at my stepmother's security and investigations firm. She's a total bad ass. She's teaching me about the business and how to conduct investigations. It's fascinating."

"That's really cool. Have you worked any cases yet?"

Selena frowned. "Not really. Martina insists being an investigator is dangerous and she's making me do a bunch of weapons and self-defense training before she'll let me go into the field, but I have learned how to review oodles and oodles of records and video footage. It's not exactly fun."

His eyes sparkled. "Wow. That is really cool. I think more women should know self-defense. Before I left for college, I made sure my sister, she's a sophomore in high school, knew how to defend herself. We used to practice together."

Huh. I did not expect that. Still. No. No, boyfriends. School. Career. Staying alive. "That's smart and cool that you look out for your sister. What do you plan to do with a degree in Political Science?"

He set down his beer on the counter behind him before turning to face her again. "I want to become a lawyer and then enter politics. Our justice system is so whacked, I want to make real changes, you know? I think the only way to do that is to know the law and then get into a position to be able to implement changes."

He was cute ...

No. No. No boyfriends. Selena, don't be fooled by a bright smile and noble future plans. "That's great. Who knows—maybe our future-career-selves will cross paths one day—" Selena lost her train of thought at the sound of vomiting followed by a room full of "eww." She turned to her left and saw the long blond hair. *Of course.* She eyed Brendon and said, "Looks like duty calls. Sorry. It was nice talking to you," before hurrying over to Dee to usher her back to their dorm room. It had been nice talking to him.

No, Selena. No boyfriends.

2

A few weeks later, Selena stood in front of the refrigerator with the door open contemplating what to have for a midnight snack. Cereal? A turkey sandwich? Yes. She pulled out a loaf of whole wheat bread and set it on the counter of her kitchenette and then went back to fish out the rest of the condiments. She hummed along to the radio while she lathered the bread with mayo and spicy mustard before topping it with sliced turkey, pickles, Monterey Jack, and tomatoes. Martina had drilled into her the importance of a healthy diet while in training—but c'mon, she was eighteen. Wasn't this the time in her life to eat pizza and cookies for dinner? Not that there were many healthy options in the cafeteria, except for the salad bar. It was one of the reasons Martina and Dad had recommended she apply to get into the Towers, where the dorms were more like apartments equipped with a kitchenette, dining table, and living room so that her diet and lifestyle could keep in check. She still ate pizza and cookies, just not for every meal.

She grabbed a bag of bbq chips from the cupboard and set them and the sandwich down at the dining table next to her laptop and Statistics book. She tore open the bag, pulled out a chip, and crunched down on the sweet and spicy goodness. She polished off the bag before eating her deluxe turkey sammy. Martina wouldn't have approved of the chips, but what she didn't know wouldn't hurt her, right?

Selena munched on her sandwich as she reviewed the details of a case that Martina sent for her to review before going into the office the next day. More video surveillance to sift through—fun. More call logs—double fun. Was Martina trying to bore her out of going into the field of private investigations? Selena was eager to take on a real case. Where she'd go out on a stakeout and help take down the bad guys, find missing persons, or provide security for people in danger. The exciting stuff. Despite being paid, Selena felt more like an intern than a member of the investigative team. *Grunt work.* Martina insisted that patience was a virtue and that it was an invaluable skill in her world. Selena polished off her sandwich and shut her laptop lid.

She pulled her notebook and Statistics book in front of her. Ten more problems left before she could call it a night. She didn't really mind. She loved college life. The freedom to come and go as she pleased. The apartment. The classes. The interesting people. People. Person. Brendon. *No, Selena, don't go there. You know better.*

Brendon Vale lived only a few doors down, and they'd often run into each other in the hall. She'd been sucked into more than a few conversations with him over the last few weeks. She knew she was developing a crush on him but was attempting to bury it deep down into a place that couldn't be accessed by anyone. She couldn't trust him, no matter how nice, sweet, funny, cute, or smart he seemed. She allowed herself one more thought of his bright smile before returning her focus to the math problems.

Selena yawned and stretched her arms out. *Last problem done.* She was about to shut the book and head to bed when the door lock jingled. Selena's body went rigid and ready for a fight. She'd eased up on grabbing for a weapon each time she heard a noise due to the fact she'd startled Dee on enough occasions that it had warranted a difficult conversation between the two of them. Selena had agreed to chill out a little bit in exchange for Dee not complaining to the Resident Advisor.

Dee pushed the door open in her usual drunken fashion with a curtain of blond hair covering her face. Selena had lived with Dee for just over two months and she still didn't understand how Dee managed to ace her science classes and party several times a week. Not that Selena struggled with her grades; the opposite, really. She thought her classes were far too easy. She couldn't wait to start taking more challenging courses. "Hey, Dee. How was the party?"

Dee glanced up. Her faced was wet and smeared with black mascara. Her once-peach colored sweater had dirt smudged on the front and was torn at the shoulder.

Selena's mouth dropped open and she jumped out of her chair. "Oh my god, are you okay? What happened?"

Dee buried her face into her hands and broke down into sobs.

Selena rushed to put her arms around her roommate. "It's okay. What happened? Let's sit over on the couch, okay?" Selena guided Dee to sit down and face her. Selena's heart pounded as she waited for Dee to explain.

Dee wiped her cheeks with the back of her hands. "I was at the party at the Delta Kappa Alpha house and, and then this guy I was talking to offered to walk me back but then as soon as we were outside he started kissing me and then pushed me down onto the ground and he pinned me down while he put on a condom and then he—you know and I didn't know him and I tried to get up and then he pushed me over onto my stomach and ..." Dee fell back into a fit of sobs.

Rage filled Selena. *This is why you can't trust men. They think they can have and do whatever they want.* She put her hand on Dee's shoulder. She didn't know what to say. She knew there wasn't anything she could say to make her feel better in that moment. Dee pushed her hair out of her face and stared at Selena. "Why did he do that? I told him I didn't want to. I told him."

Selena shook her head. "Cause he's a scumbag asshole monster. Let me get you a towel okay?"

Dee nodded.

Selena ran across the room to the bathroom and jetted back with a box of tissues and a moistened hand towel. Selena said, "Here," and handed the items to Dee.

"Thanks." Dee blew her nose and then scrubbed her face with the towel.

Selena watched Dee. She could tell she was still tipsy. "You said you didn't know the guy?"

"No, not really. I talked to him and he'd given me a drink and then we were outside. I don't remember his name."

"When did it happen?"

"Not long ago. Just now. After he was done. He left me there in the grass by the frat. He didn't even say anything, he just left. I put my clothes on and walked back here."

"You haven't gone to the police? Or the hospital?"

Dee cocked her head. "The police?"

"He raped you. You should report it to the police."

She shook her head. "I don't know if I can. They probably won't believe me. There wasn't anyone else around."

"It doesn't matter. He assaulted you. If you don't tell

anyone, he'll do it to someone else. The monsters don't stop until someone stops them." Selena's body shook at the memory of her own experience with her ex-now-dead-boyfriend, Zeek. She'd never told Dee about the experience. She hadn't told anyone at school. She was too ashamed for allowing it to happen to her, despite what her therapist continued to tell her. That it wasn't her fault. That she couldn't have known. She still felt stupid for not seeing it sooner. She knew it wasn't her fault, yet the shame remained. Maybe one day she'd be in a place where she could talk about it, but today wasn't that day.

"I just—I want to—I don't know. Maybe take a shower and try to forget the whole thing."

Selena stared into her eyes. "I know this is hard. Trust me—I know. I think you should go to the police. You will feel horrible if this guy does this to another girl and you didn't do anything to stop him. I'll go with you. I'll be your bodyguard."

Dee grabbed another tissue and wiped her nose. "You'll go with me?"

"Yes. I'll be there for you each step of the way. There will be a physical exam too. The exam is lengthy, but it's important to collect physical evidence. We should go to the hospital first and then call the police from there, okay?" Selena hadn't actually participated in a rape exam because her attacker was dead, but she'd learned about the process from Martina as part of training her for a case where a rape victim was trying to find her attacker when the police had given up on the case. Selena knew preserving evidence would be important for prosecution of the scumbag who did this to Dee. It made her so angry she could spit.

Dee nodded. "Okay, let's do it. For the other women."

"You're very brave—you know that, right?"

Dee seemed to contemplate that.

Selena encouraged her. "You can do this. You are strong. You are brave. We are going to take this guy down, okay?"

Dee inhaled and exhaled. "Okay. I can do this."

Selena stood up and said, "I'll get my keys."

"I'm gonna pee and then I'll be ready."

Selena stopped and turned to her. "Can you wait until we get to the hospital? It's full of evidence."

Dee shut her eyes and reopened them. "I can wait."

Selena knew what Dee was about to experience would be extremely unpleasant. The exam. Telling her story to strangers. The look on Dee's face said that she was beginning to understand that as well.

3

DEE

Dee wrapped her sweater across her chest. This was the very worst night of her life. She had never felt more humiliated, or more like a nonhuman. She'd been plucked, clipped, and swabbed. The nurse had been very nice and tried to console her. But it hadn't helped. She'd begun to feel like the shell of her former self.

She wasn't sure she had the strength to go with Selena to the police station and go over all the details of her attack again. Maybe she should've told the nurse to have the police meet her there at the hospital. When the nursed asked her, she just wanted to get the exam over with, and having to talk to the police seemed like a monumental chore she didn't have the energy for. She'd already had to explain to the nurse what happened and the idea of having to go over the gory details to a police officer seemed beyond her capability. It was nearly four in the morning and she was exhausted in a way that she'd never been exhausted before. It was like every inch of her body just wanted to give up. She wanted to go home and hide in her bed. She climbed off of the hospital bed, ready to leave the exam room, when the nurse said, "You did a great job and what you're doing is very brave."

Dee tried to give her a smile but was sure it came out more like a grimace. She didn't have the energy to pretend to agree with the nurse. She didn't feel brave. She felt stupid. She knew she partied more than she should, but she'd thought that's what college life was all about. Meeting new people and having exciting new experiences. She'd grown up in a strict religious household. Alcohol and being out after eleven wasn't allowed. When she arrived at San Francisco University, she finally had the freedom to let loose and go a little wild. *Live a little.* She never in a million years would've dreamed this would've happened to her. How could she have let it happen? She wanted to crawl under a rock and die. She exited the room and walked down the hall.

She eyed Selena sitting in the waiting room reading something on her phone. Dee couldn't believe her roommate had sat there for three and a half hours while she had been poked and prodded. She supposed she lucked out in the roommate department. Dee shuffled toward Selena. Selena glanced up from her phone with sadness in her eyes. "How are you? Are you okay?"

No, she wasn't okay. She'd been sexually assaulted. Raped. Victimized. Sodomized. And if that wasn't bad enough, she'd had all of her orifices swabbed and collected. She had gone from being a strong, independent female to a piece of evidence. "I'm fine."

Selena stood up. "Are you ready to head over to the university police station?"

Dee frowned. "Do we have to go tonight? The evidence has been collected. I mean, I can report it tomorrow, right? Is it important we go tonight?"

Selena shrugged. "We can call and have them meet us here,

if you prefer? I don't know, you'll probably remember the most details tonight. If it were me, I think I'd just want to get it over with, but it's totally up to you. The sooner you report him, the sooner they can prevent him from doing this to someone else."

In that moment, Dee wasn't caring too much about anybody else. Maybe this was her fault. If she hadn't been drinking, smoking, trying to get the attention of some stupid frat guy, maybe this wouldn't have happened.

Selena must've sensed her hesitation. She said, "You don't have to do anything you don't want to do. But chances are this guy will do this again to someone else. It's not like he *might* do it again. It's that he is more likely than not to do this again. Rape isn't just about sex, it's about power. You never know, maybe the next person he does something worse to, like kills them. Or maybe the next person is too scared to go to a hospital and they get an STD or become pregnant."

Kills them? She stared at Selena with bewilderment. Dee could tell Selena was really trying to do the right thing. But how could Selena possibly know what this was like? Would she have gone to the police right away? Would she have subjected herself to the invasive exam? She supposed it didn't matter. Maybe Selena was right, it would be better to just get it over with. "Fine. Let's just go to the station, that way we're closer to the dorm."

On the drive back to campus to report the attack to SFU police, Dee stared out the window of Selena's car window. She didn't feel like talking, that would require too much energy. All she could do was replay the events in her mind. She hadn't screamed. She had frozen. She was nearly six feet tall and fit. Why didn't she fight? Why had she frozen? It was as if she were a weak, frightened animal.

Selena pulled into a space in the parking garage, engaged the parking brake, and turned off the engine. She turned to face

Dee. "I want you to know, I think you're really brave for doing this. I know how hard this can be."

Dee was really tired of being told how brave she was. She sure as hell didn't feel brave. She snapped at Selena, "How could you?" She realized she shouldn't lash out with the one person who was being nice to her right now, but it was too late now.

Selena rested the keys in her lap and looked down, before looking back up. "I do know. Last year, my, uh, boyfriend raped me. It was sorta different—but it was really bad, and I didn't know if I was going to live or if I was going to die. I don't want to get into details right now, but know that I do know."

Tears were forming in Selena's eyes. Dee's body went rigid. She hadn't expected that. She now felt bad for making Selena talk about it. It was obviously still very painful to her. Maybe that's why she'd always been so quiet. "Did you go to the police and report your attacker too?" Dee asked.

Selena took a big breath in then let it out. "It was a little bit different situation, but the police were involved. They actually saved me."

"So your attacker's in jail?"

Selena's face went still and a single tear fell from her eye. "He was killed. The officer that arrived at the scene shot him so that he wouldn't shoot me." Selena wiped the tear away with the back of her hand.

Dee couldn't help but stare at Selena. *My God, what this girl has been through.* No wonder she was so adamant about Dee reporting her attacker. Selena's attacker almost killed her. "Thank you for telling me, Selena. It's so hard to talk about. I know that now."

Selena nodded. "Yeah, it really is. I have a counselor that I see and that's helped, and working with my stepmom at her security firm has helped me to become stronger and more vigilant. I'm in a better position if I were to be attacked again."

Dee now understood why Selena had always been on guard when she'd walk through the door. She had thought maybe Selena was kind of a nut job, but now she understood. Maybe she should tell her it would be okay to have the baton out again. Maybe it would save both of them.

Dee opened the door and said, "Okay, let's get this over with."

They walked across campus to the university police department. The chilly breeze felt good against her skin. A lump formed in her throat as they stepped through the automatic glass doors and made their way up to the community service officer at the front desk. Selena said under her breath, "You've got this, Dee."

Dee spoke slowly. "I need to report a sexual assault."

The young man, with black-rimmed glasses too large for his face, said, "Okay. May I have your name please?"

"Dee Hankel."

"Go ahead and take a seat over there on the chairs and an officer will be out shortly to talk with you."

She mumbled thanks and sat on wooden chairs along the wall. She turned to Selena, who sat next to her. "He said the officer will come out soon. Thank you for coming with me. I'm not sure I could've done this alone."

"No problem. Anything you need, I'm here."

Dee played with the string on her sweater, pulling it until a small hole formed.

A few minutes later, she heard footsteps approaching. Her eyes stared up. The officer was tall with a thick porn star mustache. *Gross.* "Are you Dee Hankel?"

Her heart raced. "Yes."

"Why don't you follow me into the back, and I'll take your statement."

Dee glanced over her shoulder, back at Selena. "You'll be out here?"

"I'm not going anywhere."

Dee nodded and hoisted herself off the chair using the arm rests for support. She followed the officer to a door and stopped. He swiped a security badge and opened the door. He held it open for her to enter. She entered the small room with three chairs and a desk with a computer and phone on top. It was stuffy and warm. He sat down and said, "Please have a seat."

She sat and stared at him.

"My name is Detective Grayson. Go ahead and write down your name and contact information here." He pushed a notepad and number two pencil across the desk to her.

When she was finished, she sat back in her chair.

"Great. Now, Ms. Hankel, why don't you go ahead and tell me what happened. From the beginning."

She told him what had happened in the side yard, next to the Delta Kappa Alpha house. As she recounted the details, her body shook and her speech was stammered. It was almost as if she was reliving those terrifying moments. She'd prefer to never have to think about it again, but that seemed impossible. Tears poured down her cheeks.

The officer didn't try to console her or tell her she was doing a great job. He barely even looked at her as he scribbled notes onto a notepad. When Dee finished, the officer glanced up at her. "Is that it?"

She nodded. "Yeah."

He handed her a box of tissues from atop the desk. She plucked a few tissues and blew her nose before she wiped her face clean. She was sure she looked a mess.

The officer tapped his pen on the notepad. "And you say you didn't know the man who did this? You don't even know his name?"

"No."

"But he gave you alcohol?"

"Yes."

"How many had you had?"

She averted her gaze. "I don't know. Four, maybe five."

He scribbled more notes. "You say he kissed you first—did you consent to that?"

Her eyes grew wide. "Yes, but not to the other stuff."

His eyes narrowed and with a look of skepticism, he said, "I see." He jotted a few more things on the paper before handing her his card from across his desk. "Here's my card, if you can remember anything else. I'll be in touch."

"That's it? I'm done now?"

"Yes, like I said I'll be in touch, but don't hesitate to call if you need anything or if you have any questions."

She stood up. "Okay, thank you." She turned the knob on the door and met Selena at the chairs. "I'm done."

Selena cocked her head. "Already?"

"Yep." She wasn't sure what she'd been expecting. A promise to catch the guy?

"You okay?"

Dee shrugged. "As okay as I'll be. Ready to go?"

"Uh-huh."

They trekked back across campus to their dorm room in silence. Selena reached the door and unlocked it before entering. Dee had never noticed before how Selena inspected the room before she walked through it. Selena's vigilance never seemed to falter.

Dead tired, Dee made a straight shot for the bathroom and turned on the shower. She placed her fingertips under the spout until the water turned hot. She stripped down and stepped into the shower. She cried as the hot stream washed down the front of her body. As she sobbed, she said a silent prayer. *God, if you're listening, please catch the bastard who did this. Please don't let him hurt anyone ever again. Please make what happened to me be the reason it doesn't happen to someone else.* She sniffled and wiped her eyes before grabbing the loofa. She scrubbed and scrubbed, but she wasn't sure she'd ever get clean.

4

Selena sat on the edge of her bed and zipped up her knee-high boots. She grabbed her red plaid scarf and wrapped it around her neck before standing up and tucking her baton into her front jean pocket. She never left the dorm or anywhere without her expandable baton. Fifteen ounces of stainless steel would ensure she was never a victim again. *Ever.*

At times she had thought maybe she was being paranoid, always carrying the weapon to protect herself. But as she glanced across the room at her roommate who had barely left her bed since the early morning, Selena knew she wasn't being overly cautious. She was thinking smart. Predators were everywhere. They were at parties, in hallways, and lurking around every corner. That was the thing about today's monsters—they tended to hide in plain sight. Until all the monsters were defeated, she would be ready for a fight.

Selena was fairly certain Dee wasn't asleep, considering it was three in the afternoon. She walked over to the bed and tapped Dee on the shoulder. Dee rolled herself over and looked up at her. Her eyes were red-rimmed and bloodshot. Selena said,

"I'm going to work. Do you want me to get you anything while I'm out? I should be home around nine."

Dee responded, but it was barely audible.

"I'm sorry, what was that?" Selena asked.

Dee mumbled a bit louder. "No, I'm fine."

Selena didn't think she was fine at all. She really didn't know what to do either. She knew after her own experience, she hadn't wanted to talk about it, so she hadn't pressed Dee. But she wondered if she should be trying to get help for her roommate, like recommending a counselor or a support group. She just wasn't sure what to do in this situation. She didn't want to make Dee's suffering any worse.

"Okay, well I'll be home around nine. Just text me or call me if you need anything if you change your mind."

Selena noticed a slight nod of Dee's head before she shut her eyes and turned back over onto her other side, facing the wall. Selena grabbed her coat and exited the dorm. The door shut softly behind her. In the hall she locked the deadbolt.

She felt awful for her roommate. She understood what it felt like to lose your sense of security. To be afraid to shut your eyes, because if you open them maybe your attacker would return. She shook her head and headed down the hall. She stopped cold when she heard her name being called. She pivoted back around. A slight smile formed on her cherry lips. "Oh, hey." She really needed to stop talking to this guy. Her crush grew each time they met.

Brendon jogged toward her. "Hey. I didn't see you in class this morning. Is everything okay?"

"I'm fine. It was a late night. I slept through my alarm, but I should go because I'm off to work."

Brendon put his hands in his front pockets and looked down. "Okay, cool. I just wanted to say hi. If you need notes from English, you can borrow mine."

She knew he liked her, but she also knew that they couldn't be anything more than just acquaintances. She wasn't ready to trust anybody again, especially not after what happened to Dee. "That would be great. Maybe we'll catch up later. I have to go."

"All right. See you later. Have a good time at work." He said with a wave of his hand.

She tipped her head back. "See you later." She felt sorry for herself in that moment. She wished she could be a carefree teen who saw a cute boy she liked and could just go on a date with him. She now understood the old adage, *Ignorance is Bliss*. But that wasn't her fate. She knew the horrors of what was out there and how those seemingly nice and friendly guys could in fact be sadistic killers.

Selena opened the door to Drakos Monroe Security and Investigations. Her boots made clomping noises on the marble tile as she approached the receptionist, Mrs. Pearson, an older woman who wore the brightest pink lipstick Selena had ever seen. In a cheery tone, Mrs. Pearson said, "Hi there, Selena. How are you today?"

"I'm good. Thanks. You?"

"Great. Martina wanted me to tell you she's in a last-minute session and will have to push back your meeting by thirty minutes."

"Got it. Thanks." She waved as she strolled past the front desk and into the cubical farm that contained thirty cubicle desks and two break areas. It wasn't unusual for Martina to have emergency meetings and have to push their one-on-ones. Martina was a full partner at the firm, which had come with longer hours and more responsibilities. Selena continued on to her cubicle and dropped her messenger bag on the desk before removing her coat and scarf and placing them on the back of her chair. She plopped down on her seat and powered up the computer.

She slumped over as she sifted through her emails before heading into the records room to retrieve today's files for her to review. She unlocked the cabinet with her key and pulled open the drawer. She flipped through the files until she found the one she needed, grabbed it, and relocked the cabinet.

Back at her desk, she uncapped her yellow highlighter and began to review the phone records. Today's task was to mark all incoming calls from a specific phone number. Martina had assured it was for a high-profile case that they were working, but that tidbit of information didn't make the task any less tedious. After about ten minutes, Selena's yawn practically overtook her whole body. She slid her chair back and hopped up to seek caffeine.

In the break room, she grabbed one of the graphite-colored mugs and filled it with drip coffee before adding a healthy pour of pumpkin spice creamer and a packet of sugar. Sugar and caffeine. If that didn't do the trick, nothing would.

She took a sip of the liquid energy. It wasn't as good as a Frappuccino, but it would have to do. She turned to head back to her cubicle when she heard Martina's voice. Selena swiveled back around and spotted Martina walking toward her. She was dressed in head-to-toe black and wore her dark hair cropped short. Martina was the epitome of no-nonsense. "Hey, Martina."

Martina approached and grabbed a mug for herself. "Hi Selena, sorry I had to push back our meeting. Are you okay? You look awful. Late night studying? "

The lipstick and mascara apparently weren't doing the trick to conceal her lack of sleep. "No, not studying but there was something I wanted to talk to you about. That is, if you have a few minutes—it's not work-related, but something happened last night."

"Of course. I'm done with my other meetings for the day, I'm yours for the rest of the afternoon. What happened?"

"Can we go into one of the conference rooms, it's kind of sensitive?"

Worry fell over Martina's face. "Of course."

Martina finished fixing her coffee and led Selena to a small conference room with a table and four chairs. Selena set her mug down on the table and explained to Martina what had happened to Dee in the early hours of that morning.

Martina put her hand to her chest. "How awful. I don't know if you realize this or not, but more than half of all college sexual assaults happen between August and November. I wish the dangers, especially for incoming freshman, were more widely known. First time away from home and it's easy to believe that your fellow classmates or dorm mates are your friends and are trustworthy. The sad truth is that, that isn't always the case. How is she doing?"

"Not great. That's what I wanted to talk to you about. I'm not sure how to help her. She's been in bed all day and I know how much you helped me after what happened. What do you think I should do?"

Martina gave her a reassuring smile. "The best thing you can do for her is to be there for her and listen to her. Key word is *listen*. If she wants to talk about it—listen. But if she doesn't want to talk about it, don't force it. You can recommend she see a counselor or attend a support group. I will get you some names of a few good counselors specializing in sexual assault victims as well as a few recommendations for support groups on campus. But unfortunately, beyond that, Selena, there's not really anything you can do. The most important thing, like I mentioned, is to just be there and be a good listener."

Selena wished she could do more than just listen. She'd prefer to track down the jerk who did this to Dee and beat him with her baton. *No, Selena. Too violent.* Her therapist had explained that violent thoughts were normal but told her not to act on them because despite how it sounded, it wouldn't make her feel any better.

"All right, I'll do that. I'll give her the information once you give it to me. Are you sure there's nothing else I can do? What about the police investigation? Do you know anyone at the University Police Department? Maybe you can pull some strings and get Dee's case made a priority?" Selena had seen firsthand the sway Martina had with law enforcement when they were familiar with her skills and reputation.

"Unfortunately, I don't know anyone over there. Dee gave a statement to the police, correct?"

"Yes. It took all of about five minutes. The officer gave Dee his card and said he'd be in touch."

Martina folded her arms across her chest and leaned back in her chair. "What I would do—and I'm not saying I recommend you do this—but you could follow up on the investigation on her behalf. I hesitate to say this because technically they can't tell you anything, but if you ask the right questions you should be able to get a sense for how the investigation is going and if they're actively working it."

"*If* they're working it? Why wouldn't they? She was raped!"

Martina let out a breath. "You'd be surprised. Despite the fact that one in five women will be sexually assaulted in their lifetime, most police officers I've encountered don't believe the victim. It's awful. What happens is they end up investigating the victim instead of the perpetrator. They ask questions of the victim like what were they doing when they were attacked, what were they wearing, and what is their sexual history. They don't even bother to think about what was the behavior of the attacker. It's unconscionable. Not to mention the number of rape kits that never actually get tested. California is the leading state for untested rape kits. It's an atrocity."

Selena's mouth dropped open. "They might not even test her kit? It took over three hours to collect!"

"Unfortunately, it happens."

Selena couldn't believe what she was hearing. Why would the police investigate the victim and not believe him or her? When somebody reports a robbery did the police ask, are you sure you were robbed? What were you wearing when you were robbed? Were you asking for it? No, those questions were reserved for the women and men who were sexually assaulted. *It was horrible.* As Martina continued to lecture her on all the injustices toward sexual assault victims, Selena decided right then and there she would most definitely be following up on Dee's case.

5

Selena slipped her backpack on and hurried out of the lecture hall. She only had an hour between her last class and the next and she wanted to head over to the police station to enquire about Dee's case. Selena was determined to make sure the case actually got investigated.

After Martina explained to her the previous day, what could happen, Selena knew Dee needed an advocate. Someone who would follow up with the detectives and make sure they didn't toss her file into the pile of un-investigated sexual assaults that *they* believed were either made up or women who "had changed their mind after." It made her physically ill to think about it. It was total bullshit. What woman would go through a three-hour invasive medical exam and then have to explain in gory detail a sexual act that was both violent and terrifying, if it weren't true? The concept was ridiculous. She agreed with Martina that the victim blaming needed to stop—like yesterday.

She reached the campus police department and walked up to the community service officer behind the window. She gave her best friendly looking smile. "Hi, I'd like to speak with Detective Grayson, please."

"Do you have an appointment?"

She batted her long lashes. "No, I just wanted to check up on a case."

"And what's your name?"

"Selena Bailey."

The young man with the giant glasses, pushed the black frames up over the bridge of his nose. "Alright, let me check with him. Go ahead and take a seat over there. He'll be out when he's available to see you."

"Thanks."

Selena sat herself in the seat and glanced around the office. It was a much smaller than the police department in Grapton Hill, the station she had frequented while they were investigating her mother's murder and then for a formal statement after Selena's boyfriend tried to kill her, after kidnapping and torturing her. But the smell was the same. A mixture of cleaning fluid and stale cigarettes. It was an odd mix considering it was illegal to smoke in or anywhere near the building.

A few minutes later she watched as Detective Grayson approached. He had a large presence and an overall creepy vibe to him. If he hadn't been in uniform, she'd have her hand on her baton ready for an attack. His eyes met hers. His casual and friendly demeanor soon dissipated, as if he recognized her from the previous day as the person who had come in with Dee. Selena stood up and extended her hand. "Detective Grayson, I'm Selena Bailey."

He shook her hand and retreated back with fists on his hips. "What can I do for you today, Ms. Bailey?"

"I was hoping we could talk about my roommate, Dee Hankel's case? I don't know if you remember me, but I came in with her yesterday morning with her to give her statement. As you can imagine, she's not up for classes or getting out yet. I've come down to see if there's been any progress on the case. Have you gotten results from her rape kit back yet?"

The detective's gaze shifted from left to right. "Why don't you join me in the office and we can talk."

Selena nodded and followed him into the office. She sat down in the chair and waited for Detective Grayson to get situated. Finally, after shuffling some papers and tapping on the keyboard, he said, "So what can I do for you? You said you were checking in on Dee's case?"

"Yes, I want to ask if the rape kit has been tested and if you have any suspects."

"I can't give you details of an open investigation, Ms. Bailey. But, so that you understand, it usually takes at least a month before we get results back from the lab."

Martina had warned her about this. She knew the university had the power to put in a forty-eight-hour rush on the DNA testing and fingerprinting. The fact that he was telling her that it would take over a month was indicative that they hadn't made Dee's case a high priority. It made her blood boil, but Selena was determined to remain calm—or at least appear to be calm. Getting excited wouldn't help anyone. "Why didn't you do a rush order on the testing? Are there a lot of other sexual assault cases that are a higher priority than Dee's?"

The detective pressed his lips together, and he clenched his jaw. She realized her question may have come out a bit more hostile than she was intending. She tried to remain sweet and innocent in appearance, but she was having a difficult time managing her emotions.

The officer crossed his arms across his chest and sat up straight in the chair and stared her down. Uniform or not, she didn't like this guy. He said, "I don't know what you think you know, Ms. Bailey, but our standard protocol is that we send it off to the lab and it gets processed in the amount of time it requires to be processed. I can't give out details about a suspect. And if your roommate is so interested in the investigation, why doesn't she come down herself?"

Selena couldn't believe the cold attitude of this officer, who was supposedly tasked with protecting the students. "Dee's been through a traumatic event, Detective. She's at home and she's barely left her bed. I'm here on her behalf to ensure the investigation actually gets completed and that her case is taken seriously. I did a little digging into the crime stats on college campuses across the state and it appears that they are notorious for not taking sexual assault claims seriously or not punishing students when they've been identified. And just so you know, Detective, I'm not gonna just let this go. I will be here every day until you have an update or you've closed the case—whichever comes first." Her blood boiled, but she maintained a steady breath determined to not lose her cool.

The detective leaned back and licked his lips. The gesture made Selena want to hurl, but she managed to keep her eyes fixed on his. He needed to know that she was serious and that he'd be dealing with her on a daily basis until he made some progress on the case. She watched as he seemed to contemplate his next move with her. He smirked with a gleam in his eye. "You're welcome to come down here every day, but that's not going to make this happen any faster. I'm sorry that your friend is not doing well. Please give her my regards. Let her know she's welcome to call me anytime. Now if you don't mind, I have work to do."

He stood up, towering over Selena. He wasn't likely more than six feet tall, but in that moment, he appeared to be as large as a bear. A disgusting, slimy bear. Selena grasped the chair handles and pushed herself out of the chair and picked up her backpack by one strap. She glared up at him. "Thank you for your time, Detective. I'll see you tomorrow." She didn't wait for a response. Instead she walked out of the office, head held high.

She stepped out of the station into the chilly air. Her body felt like it was on fire, so it was just the cool down she needed. She continued across campus to her next class, angry and frustrated. The meeting hadn't gone as hoped. She wanted to make a friendly alliance with the police and hopefully forge a connection, but this guy wasn't having it. What the hell?

6

DEE

Dee lay on her bed, staring up at her roommate, who was attempting to coax her out of her warm cocoon. She hadn't left their dorm room in the last week. She didn't even want to think about the mounting assignments she'd ignored and the chemistry and biology labs she probably wouldn't be able to make up. She just couldn't bring herself to leave the safety of the room *and* it was *really* cold outside. Not to mention, what if she ran into him, the guy who had attacked her? The guy who not only violated her body but also destroyed her sense of self. Dee had never thought of herself as weak or small, but this guy had changed all that. Now she was like a wilted flower afraid to leave the room for fear of being crushed or stomped on. She didn't feel like doing anything. She didn't want to talk and didn't want to go for a walk. She didn't want to do her homework or attend classes. She didn't want to do anything but try to forget, but she couldn't. She responded to Selena. "I don't want to go to the cafeteria."

"It will help you to get a little exercise—it'll get the blood flowing. It's supposed to help."

Dee was skeptical that anything would help. Selena had

been very understanding and had offered to be there for her and said she'd listen if Dee wanted to talk. She didn't want to talk. If she talked about it, it would be too real. But maybe she should try to go to dinner. She was getting sick of eating kettle chips for every meal. Not that she had much of an appetite, but maybe some comfort food could, well, be comforting. "Fine. I'll go, but I don't want to go anywhere else, okay?"

Selena held up both of her hands. "I promise. Just dinner and I'll be with you the whole time. Also, I got you something."

Dee watched as Selena went over to her backpack, unzipped the front pouch, and pulled out something that look like a big, fat pen. Dee sat up on the bed and flattened her disheveled hair with her hand. She was sure she looked atrocious.

Selena returned to the edge of Dee's bed and handed her the black shiny object. Selena said, "It looks like a pen, but really it's pepper spray. Take off the cap and you'll see."

Dee did as she was instructed and saw the spray nozzle at the top. It was strange, how something so small and innocuous seeming could have maybe prevented her attacker from doing what he did. "What do I do—just spray it in an attacker's eyes?"

"Actually, my stepmother, Martina, said that it's better if you aim for the mouth because it will mess with their respiratory system, both their throat and their nose, which could incapacitate them more than just in their eyes."

"Wow. Okay. Thank you. I like that it's sort of inconspicuous."

"Sure. You, uh, ready to go?"

It appeared that Selena was trying to suppress a frown. Dee knew she most likely looked like a cast member from *The Walking Dead*—one of the dead ones. "Let me get dressed first." She went over to her dresser and pulled out a fresh pair of jeans, a T-shirt, and her SFU sweatshirt. As she tugged on the purple sweatshirt with a bright green dragon on the center she remembered getting her acceptance email and how excited she had been to be leaving Sacramento. She was determined to not only ace her chemistry classes and get accepted into medical school, but she'd also envisioned how cool and cosmopolitan it would be to live in the city of San Francisco. She'd been having the time of her life until seven nights ago. She tucked her new pepper spray pen into her pocket and slipped on her pointed flats. She gave her hair a final pat down and faced Selena. "I'm ready."

Selena led the way out of their dorm. Selena stood in the hall waiting for Dee to join her. Dee hesitated before stepping over the threshold. Her heart rate quickened. She swallowed and glanced over at Selena. Selena gave her a look of understanding. *You can do this.* She shut and locked the door behind her.

"Are you okay?" Selena asked.

Dee nodded. "I'll be okay."

She stayed close to Selena as they headed down the hallway toward the elevators. Her back tightened. Dee's legs froze as her eyes darted around looking for any possible sign of an attacker. But the only people around were Selena and herself. Dee couldn't relax, but she moved one foot in front of the other. She wanted turn around and run back, knowing that as soon as they reached the cafeteria, at this time of night, it would be bustling with students. Students who may try to attack her. She was nearly certain her attacker was a member of the DKA house and a student at the university. He could be anywhere. He could be in one of her classes or waiting in the cafeteria. She put her hand on her pepper spray pen in her pocket as they entered the cafeteria and stood in line for the daily special. *Tacos.* Dee hadn't eaten much in the last week, and the smell of the spicy ground beef and cheddar cheese was heavenly. Her stomach grumbled. She was getting all the fixings. And dessert.

Food entrées received and meal cards swiped, Selena and Dee sat at a table away from most of the crowd. Selena gave her a sheepish grin. "Are you doing okay?"

Despite the thumping in her chest, Dee said, "Yeah. Did you, uh, after your incident, did you have a hard time going out?"

Selena dropped her gaze. "It was hard. Thankfully, it was the worst and best situation. Because of what happened, I was reunited with my father and met my stepmom. I moved in with them immediately after I was released from the hospital—before that I was living with my boyfriend, the one who kidnapped me and attacked me and then tried to kill me." Selena's eyes met Dee's. "I didn't go to school for weeks. Luckily, it mostly fell during winter break, but even then, I took a little bit of extra time and went on independent study. I was also lucky to have my stepmother, who knows a lot about this kind of stuff. She found me a therapist right away. She also found me a support group close by. I was talking to her about what happened to you and she suggested, if you want to—no pressure—but that it might help to see a counselor or go to a support group here on campus. She gave me the names of some good counselors in the area and then also told me about a support group right here on campus. Apparently, there is a center on campus that has counselors and all kinds of support for victims of sexual violence. It's really cool, actually. I was thinking about going myself because even though it's been almost a year since the attack, I still get flashbacks and am still probably more on edge than I should be. The support group really helps, and I haven't been to one since school started. It helps to be around people who have been through a similar situation. It makes you feel a little less alone. I plan to go next week. You can join me if you want, but no pressure."

Dee let that sink in. If she went to a counselor, would her parents find out? She was still on their insurance. She knew it would kill them if they knew what had happened to her. Support group, maybe? It would be nice to have someone like Selena to go with for the first time, it would seem less scary. "I'll think about it."

She bit down on her taco and it was like a flavor explosion in her mouth. The melted cheese mixed with sour cream, tomato, and beef was amaze-balls. She quickly devoured the first taco before she slowed herself down.

She wanted to ask Selena more questions about her experience, but she didn't want to pry. She knew how hard it was to talk about her own experience. It didn't seem right to make somebody else talk about theirs. Selena was certainly on top of it when it came to her personal safety, but she seemed like she was doing okay. Maybe she just had a better exterior façade than Dee did?

They finished their meal and headed back up to their dorm room, chatting about their least favorite classes. It felt almost normal. Dee was glad she'd gotten out. It felt good. They strolled down the hall toward their room when Dee's heart nearly stopped. The voice. She'd heard it before. She looked ahead and saw him.

Selena waved. "Hi, Brendon."

"Hey. How are you? Hi, Dee."

Dee stood frozen.

Brendon gave her a peculiar look and continued. "This is my friend, Tyler. Tyler, this is Selena and this is Dee. Two of the coolest chicks on our floor." He winked at Selena.

Dee stared at Tyler with his bleached blond hair and surfer tan. His icy blue eyes.

Selena said, "It's nice to meet you, Tyler." Selena glanced over her shoulder and Dee met her gaze. Selena's face fell.

Dee stated, "I'm not feeling well. I have to go now."

Selena turned back around and told Brendon, "We should get going. It's good to see you. Nice to meet you, Tyler."

They waved goodbye as Dee hurried to their door. Her keys jingled in her hands as she attempted to unlock the door, but instead the keys fell out of her hands onto the floor. Selena caught up and opened the door with her own key.

Dee grabbed her keys and ran inside and shut the door behind both of them rather abruptly. Selena's eyes were wide. "What's wrong?"

Her body was shaking. "That was him. Tyler. It was Tyler."

Selena's mouth dropped open. "Are you sure?"

"Positive." He was twenty feet from her room. Her bed. Her home.

7

Seated next to Dee on the couch, Selena asked, "You're absolutely sure Tyler was the person who attacked you?"

Dee dabbed her eyes with a tissue. "It's him. The voice. The face. It was definitely him."

"Do you recognize the name Tyler? Can you think of his last name?"

"It doesn't sound wrong, but I don't know a last name. It's all so fuzzy. But I know it's him."

Selena contemplated what the next move could be. She could easily get information on Tyler from Brendon, but she'd need to be careful to not raise any suspicions with Brendon. Brendon seemed like an okay guy, but you never know. If he was friends with a guy like that, he probably wasn't any better. Thank goodness she hadn't let herself go for him. She still couldn't distinguish the monsters from the good guys. "Are you okay if I leave you here so that I can go and talk to Brendon to find out more information about Tyler?"

Dee's eyes flashed open. "What if he's still out there? What if they both attack you? It's not safe, Selena. It's not safe."

Adrenaline was soaring through Selena. She concealed her

shaking hands from Dee by putting them in her coat pockets. "I'll be fine. I've got my baton and I've had nine months of self-defense training. They should be afraid of me." Sometimes Selena wondered if talking the talk would actually make her tougher. She had indeed been in training for nine and a half months and she thought she could handle an attack, but you never know. Tyler was a big guy, but it wasn't likely that he would attack her in the hallway, but behind closed doors, that was a different story. And what about Brendon? He was bigger than Selena, probably stronger, and she knew he had training from working with his sister. She had her baton and the element of surprise. She'd be fine, right?

"The real question is, are you okay with me leaving you right now? I can stay here and talk to Brendon tomorrow."

She really wanted to find out more about this Tyler guy now. The more she knew, the more she could tell the police, but she also didn't want to leave Dee if she was in too fragile of a state.

Selena watched as Dee pulled her new pepper spray pen out of her pocket. "I'll be okay. Just make sure you lock the door and I'll stay in the back room."

Selena could tell that Dee was terrified, but she would just be down the hall for a quick conversation. She'd be back in two shakes of a lamb's tail. Or whatever that saying was. Selena stood up and patted her pocket with the baton. "I'll be back really soon. Call me if anything spooks you. We're going to catch this guy and he's gonna pay for what he did." Selena would make sure of it.

Dee didn't respond but leaned back into the couch. Selena grabbed the keys from the coffee table and exited the dorm room, shutting and locking the door behind her. She'd need to be quick. She strutted down the hall to Brendon's dorm room. She approached the door and knocked three times in quick succession.

Butterflies flew around furiously in her stomach as she waited for Brendon to open the door. She hated he had this effect on her. She needed to squash this little crush she had on him and pronto. No good could come out of this. He was friends with a sexual predator for God's sake. This visit was strictly business, not personal. The door opened and Brendon gave her a wide smile. "Well, this is a surprise."

She forced herself to remain straight-faced. No, she needed to be friendly. If she were serious, he'd wonder why. She needed to get better at this. She smiled. "Hey, I just want to come by and say hi. Is your friend Tyler still here?"

She watched his body language and he seemed to stiffen. Did he not want her to see Tyler? He let his hand fall from the edge of the door and leaned against the wall. "No, sorry, he left a while ago. It's just me." His smile had faded.

Ahh. He thought that she was interested in Tyler. *Dammit.* She'd need to come up with a better reason to be talking to Brendon about Tyler than her own interest. She really hadn't thought this all the way through. "Oh, I was just with Dee and she said she thinks she recognized him from back home in Sacramento. I think she's interested in him, but she's not feeling great, so I thought I'd say hi and make an inquiry on her behalf. Silly girl stuff, I know." She giggled and tossed her hair, hoping to become more believable, and not appear to be on an investigative endeavor. She wasn't sure she was pulling it off.

He stepped back. "You want to come in?"

"Sure." Was this a bad idea? She rubbed the baton in her pocket. *I'll be fine.* She entered his dorm room and it was the mirror image of Dee's and her apartment-style dorm room. "Is your roommate here?"

"No, he's out studying. Can I get you anything to drink, maybe?"

Selena wrinkled her nose. "I don't drink."

"Not even water? Or soda? You must be so dehydrated. That can't be healthy," he teased.

She could tell he wanted this to be a social visit, so she'd need to play along. She didn't want to have to tell him the real story and lose out on valuable information. "Ha. Ha. I'll have a soda."

His eyes lit up. "Coming right up. Coke okay?"

"Sure." Soda was not on her list of approved dietary items from Martina, but it was for a good cause. *Justified.* She stood in the living room while Brendon grabbed two sodas from the refrigerator. He turned around with a can in each hand and said, "Would you like to sit on the couch?"

"Okay." Selena kinda knew where this was going. Her and him on a sofa, next to each other, drinking sodas. She looked into his eyes. They seem to be kind and warm, but she couldn't trust her instincts—not yet. She hoped one day, but today was not that day.

She sat down on the brown sofa and he handed her the soda can. She took a sip and enjoyed the slow burn down her throat. She let out an, "ahh," Oh, how she'd missed the burn followed by an intense sugar rush. Martina insisted a strong, healthy body was a strong, healthy mind.

Brendon sat next to her. He laughed at her obvious enjoyment of the carbonated beverage. "So, how have you been? You seem to be pretty busy these days."

She set the soda down on his coffee table and said, "Um, good." *Good like, I've been going to the police station every day, multiple times a day trying to get updates on the case, but Detective Grayson now refuses to see me.* She was sure she'd been flagged. Since the first day she went on her own, it had been the same thing. He'd send a message to the officer at the front desk and tell her that there was no new news and to basically go away.

"Between work and school and everything, I've kinda kept to myself. How have you been?"

"Same old, same old. School. Class. Parties."

"Like partying with Tyler?" Was that nonchalant? She didn't think so.

"Sometimes with Tyler at the DKA house. They pretty much have a party there every single night. I don't know how those guys get any sleep."

"Oh, are you part of Delta Kappa Alpha?" She hadn't pegged Brendon for a frat guy, but he did want to go into politics.

He shook his head vigorously. "Oh no, I'm not really into the frat scene. I met Tyler during rush week when I was contemplating it, before I saw what actually goes on in those houses. Plus the cost and time commitment. Not the right fit for me."

"But you still hang out with Tyler?"

"Yeah, from time to time. He's cool."

Selena was beginning to think Brendon was not a great judge of character. "What's Tyler's last name? I was supposed to find out. Roommate's orders." That was more natural, right?

Brendon tipped his head as if thinking that it was an odd question. *Pretty please, tell me.* She gave a warm smile.

He smiled back. "It's King."

"Tyler King? Do you know if he's from Sacramento?" *Okay, I'm getting the hang of this now.*

"No, I think he's from Calabasas, down in southern California."

Check and check. "Oh. Okay, he must not be the same person that Dee thought she knew. Okay, well then, I should go, it's getting late."

She was about to stand up when Brendon put his hand on her leg and gazed into her eyes. "Do you have to leave?"

Her body tensed. "Dee wasn't feeling well, and I want to check on her."

Brendon removed his hand and sat back. "I'm just going to say this. I'll probably regret it later, but I feel like you and I have this great connection. You're beautiful and you're smart and you're tough and I really like you. I get the feeling you like me too, but then you avoid me for days. I don't understand."

She froze at his confession. In his warm, brown eyes was hurt and confusion. Selena averted her gaze. She couldn't look at him. She did like him. She wished she could let herself tell him. To be able to trust him. She didn't want to not trust him, but she didn't. She couldn't trust him or herself. She exhaled heavily. "It's not you, Brendon, it's me. I have some weird things going on and I just can't right now. I just can't." Why did she say *not right now*? She didn't mean that. Did she?

His eyes pleaded with her. "Are you sure? It's not something I did?"

He was really tugging at the heartstrings now. Maybe he was a good guy. Maybe she should talk to her counselor about him. She wanted to have a real relationship someday, but she wasn't ready to trust again. And Brendon was connected to Tyler, so who knew? She couldn't make the same mistake again. Being alone would be far less painful than that. "I have a lot going on right now. I'm sorry. I have to go." She stood up and hurried out of his apartment and rushed back to her dorm room. She unlocked the dead bolt and opened the door, closing it quickly behind her.

She leaned against the door and shut her eyes. She took some cleansing breaths in and out. Oh, what she would give to be normal. She opened her eyes and saw Dee staring at her as if she was some sort of weird alien. "Did something happen?" she blurted.

"I got his last name. His name is Tyler King and he's from Calabasas."

Dee grabbed her phone and furiously tapped into it. She mumbled, "Fucking asshole jerk face."

Selena nearly smiled. Angry Dee was far better than sad Dee. She watched over Dee's shoulder as she pulled up information on her phone. Dee scrolled through Tyler's social media accounts. She'd found him. Now they had a name and a photo. They had everything they needed to bring to the police so that they could arrest him.

8

_____

Selena and Dee stood in front of the same community service officer at the front desk of the university police station. Selena said, "We're here to see Detective Grayson. We have additional evidence in the case to share with him."

Selena gave Dee a reassuring smile as she watched Dee chew on her fingernails. It was a new habit that Dee had picked up in the last week since the attack. It wasn't surprising that Dee was on edge. Selena was usually on edge too, and it had almost been a year since her ordeal. She was less fearful, but definitely still on edge. Her counselor said that in time it would get better. It hadn't yet. "And you are?" the receptionist asked.

Seriously, what was with this guy? Selena had been there every day for the last week. "I'm Selena Bailey and this is Dee Hankel."

"I'll let them know you're here. Please have a seat."

She rolled her eyes at the guy and motioned for Dee to come sit on the chairs with her. Dee sat hunched over, chewing on the nail of her pointer finger. Selena put her hand on her shoulder. "It'll be okay. He needs to pay for what he did. Are you okay?"

Dee nodded nervously.

"Do you want to talk about it?" Selena asked.

"No, it's fine. I just want to get this over with."

"Okay." Selena checked her email on her phone to stop herself from bugging Dee.

A few minutes later, the detective approached with a smirk on his face. "Ladies, what can I help you with today?"

Selena said, "Dee has identified the attacker. We have a name and photo."

The detective glanced at Dee and then back at Selena with skepticism in his eyes. "Ms. Hankel, if you have new information, how about you follow me back into the office area and we can discuss it."

Dee turned to look at Selena.

Selena popped up and stood with her hands on her hips. "I'll be coming with her."

Selena had learned from Martina that it was more than acceptable to have a friend or family member accompany the victim when discussing the case. Selena feared that Detective Porn-stache would try to bully Dee with a condescending tone, or more aggressively by outright telling her he didn't believe her or trying to convince her to drop the case. Selena would ensure everything was on the up and up. She'd be both a witness and advocate for Dee.

He shrugged. "Fine. Follow me."

They followed Detective Grayson into the office and sat in the tiny room. He mumbled, "I'll be right back," and then returned a few minutes later with a file folder in his hands. He flipped open the cover and used his index finger to skim the notes.

Selena attempted to get a better look at the notes, but he was covering too much of the text and she couldn't make it out. Ignoring Selena's presence he asked, "So you know the name of your attacker now?"

Dee stammered. "Yeah, I saw him in the hall and then we found out from a friend that his name is Tyler King. We looked him up on social media and it's the right name and the right guy."

Detective Grayson raised an eyebrow. "You just happened to run into the guy? That's pretty convenient, don't you think?"

Dee's face paled.

Selena's heart was racing, and she was fighting mad. She didn't like this guy's tone and she didn't like the implications he was making that Dee had misidentified her attacker. She could no longer hold back. "We ran into Tyler King in the hallway—steps away from our dorm room. The friend he was with is someone who lives on our floor. Now, Dee has a name, address, and a picture. There is no reason for you to treat her like she's some sort of liar."

Detective Grayson glared at Selena. "If you can't contain yourself, young lady, I'm going to need for you to leave."

She sat back, arms crossed, and chest heaving. She wanted to beat the smug look off his face.

Dee spoke slowly. "What Selena said is what happened. His name is Tyler King. This is his photo." She lifted her phone. The screen had a picture of Tyler from his Facebook profile. "This is him. This is the guy who attacked me."

Detective Grayson gave a cursory glance of the picture. "You were fairly intoxicated that night. Isn't that right? How can you be so sure that this was the person who did this to you?"

Dee pleaded and her voice cracked. "Because I remember his face and the sound of his voice. It was him. He lives at the DKA house."

Selena could tell that Dee was on the verge of tears. She wanted to shake the officer and scream at him. Why wasn't anyone listening? Selena refrained from yelling at the officer for obvious reasons.

Dee shut her eyes. "Yes, I was drinking, but I remember him. I remember his voice. I remember what he did."

The officer leaned back in his seat and stared at Dee. "And what exactly was it that he did?"

Selena had to refrain from jumping up and attacking like a feral cat. He was baiting her and trying to intimidate Dee by implicating that she wasn't credible because she had a few drinks. Selena wished somebody would sexually assault this man so he'd understood what it was like and then maybe he'd drop the callous attitude towards someone who was brutally attacked. Selena nodded to Dee.

Dee recounted every gory detail of the attack from the first drink Tyler had given her to lying next to the bushes after he was finished.

Detective Grayson didn't take any notes. "I'll update the file listing Tyler King as your reported attacker. We will bring him in for questioning. Is there anything else, Ms. Hankel?"

Dee stared at the floor. "That's it. That's all there is."

"All right, ladies, I hope you have a good night. I'll look into this. *Ms. Hankel*, give me a call if you have any questions."

Selena stared in disbelief at Detective Grayson. Up until now her experience with law enforcement had been limited to working with Detective Gates during her mother's homicide investigation and her subsequent kidnapping. Detective Gates had cared about Selena, and her mother's case. He had checked up on her daily after her mother's death. He never once spoke with her in a rough or accusatory tone. He had saved her life. Selena had thought the police were there to help, but now she was learning firsthand that wasn't true of all law enforcement.

After all Selena had been through, she had considered going into law enforcement. She thought she would be working with good people who were tasked with serving and protecting citizens, but now she wasn't so sure.

She looked at Dee. "Let's go home."

They walked silently back to their dorm. Both of them fully understanding what had just transpired. Dee had been victim blamed and her story not believed. The officer didn't even try to conceal his attitude. If they couldn't count on the police to protect them, who would?

9

Selena watched nervously as Dee paced around the dorm room with her cell phone pressed to her ear. Her eyes were wide and her arms flailing around as if she was being told something that was completely unbelievable. Dee stopped and stabbed her finger at her phone screen and then dropped it onto her bed. She slowly sat on the edge of the bed and then buried her face into her hands and sobbed. Selena jetted from the living room over to Dee. She sat next to her on the bed, her heart racing. This couldn't be good news. "What's wrong? What did he say?"

Through sobs, Dee said, "He said he talked to Tyler. Tyler said he remembered me and that we had a great night and that it was completely consensual and that he was shocked I was pressing charges." Dee's body heaved and she continued to sob.

Anger seared through Selena. Of course, that's what Tyler would say. He was a goddamn monster. He should be arrested. He should be behind bars. He shouldn't be walking around free to pick out his next victim.

She didn't want to press Dee for too many details, since it was clear she was having very difficult time with the news. Dee lifted her head and turned to Selena. "That detective said I should just drop the case and that there was no way they'd be able to prosecute him. Tyler told him that it was all my idea and that I had coaxed him outside because I liked to have rough, outdoor sex. That I got off on it and that I was really wasted. Tyler said he wasn't that into it, but that I practically begged him. Can you believe that?"

Selena's mouth dropped open. How could anyone possibly believe that Dee had asked for any of this to happen to her? It was completely outrageous. Her anger was bubbling up. She feared she would not be able to sustain a calm demeanor. She wanted to hit something. She wanted to break something. She focused on her surroundings to halt her overwhelming, raging emotions. *I'm here at San Francisco University in my dorm room. The time is seven p.m. The day is November 15. Three objects I notice around me are a bed, a desk, and a chair. Three colors I notice around me are purple, green, and yellow.*

Selena put her arm on Dee's shoulder. "I'm so sorry, Dee."

Dee shook her head. "I can't believe they don't believe me. I did that rape kit exam. I went to them right away. I did everything I was supposed to do. I don't understand. Why don't they believe me?"

Fucking patriarchy. Selena didn't know what to do, but she was not going to let this go. Tyler King was not going to get away with attacking her roommate or any other woman ever again. "I believe you. And I will make sure that Tyler pays for what he did."

Dee stared blankly at the floor. "What am I supposed to do now? He said they don't have a case, so they won't even press charges. They said it's he said, she said."

Selena fought the rage. "There is a support group meeting tonight in about an hour. It's here on campus at the Center for Victims of Sexual Violence. They have counselors and they have support groups. If you want, we can grab some dinner at the cafeteria and then head over to the meeting. It can't hurt, right?"

Dee stared at Selena. "You'll come with me?"

"Of course."

Selena gave her friend a warm hug and went into the bathroom to retrieve a box of tissues and handed them to Dee. Selena wouldn't let this go. Tyler King would not get away with what he'd done to Dee. Selena would launch her first investigation and she would obtain the evidence to prove that Tyler assaulted Dee. One way or another, Tyler would pay for what he did.

10

DEE

With Selena by her side, Dee forced herself to hold her head high as she walked through the doors to the Center for Victims of Sexual Violence. She approached a young woman sitting behind a desk in the middle of the lobby. Her nerves rattled, but she knew she couldn't let this destroy her. She needed to get help. She didn't want to feel like this anymore. Even if Tyler King was going to get away with the crime, he wasn't going to be allowed to take away her life. Or maybe she was fooling herself; maybe she'd always be afraid. "Hi, I'm here for the support group."

The young woman gave a friendly smile. "Have you been here before?"

Dee shook her head from side to side.

"My name is Kathy and I'm one of the volunteers here. If this is your first time, maybe you would also like to make an appointment with a counselor too?"

Dee wondered if what had happened to her showed on her face. Would she never be able to hide it, from herself or the rest of the world? "A counseling appointment for today?"

The woman lowered her voice. "If this is something that's

happened recently and you haven't talked to anyone yet, I would recommend setting up an appointment very soon. It's absolutely free. We can even help with going to the police or helping with your case. We're here to help in any way we can."

Selena stepped closer to the desk. "Really? You'll help with the police too?"

"Yes, we provide advocacy for all of our students. This can be a very troubling time for a lot of women and men. We have staff here that will assist with going to the police, getting an exam done, and obviously counseling and support groups too. Is this something that happened recently?"

Selena turned to look at Dee.

Dee nodded. "It happened just over a week ago. I've already reported it to the police and had the exam, but they said there isn't anything they can do. I haven't talked to anyone else yet." She could feel Selena's dainty fingers on her shoulder. She resisted the urge to break down right then and there. Every time she talked about that night it made her crumble.

The woman wrinkled up her face before giving her a tense smile. "You still have about ten minutes before the support group starts, why don't we go ahead and make you a counseling appointment?"

Dee nodded again.

"Okay." The woman slid a clipboard with a questionnaire and pen tucked under the clip, across the desk. "Go ahead and fill in your information and we'll get you into a counselor as soon as possible. We can work around your school schedule too. Are you still going to class?"

Dee picked up the clipboard but didn't look the woman in the eyes. "I haven't gone since the … since it happened."

"Okay, I will get you an appointment right away. And from my own experience, I can tell you, I think the support group will help." The woman eyed Selena. "Are you here for support group too, or are you here as a friend?"

Selena said, "I'm here for the support group. My assault happened almost a year ago. I have a counselor that I see regularly, but this is my first time at a support group here on campus."

The young woman's hazel eyes sparkled. "Great, glad to have you. Most of the women here at the center are volunteers. A lot of us are volunteers because we know what you're going through and we want to help and give back. So if you have any questions at all, don't hesitate to reach out to any of us."

Selena said, "Thank you."

Dee finished filling in her contact information and handed the clipboard back to the woman. As the woman tapped her keyboard and studied her screen, Dee turned to Selena. "Here goes."

"It's gonna be hard at first, but in the end, I think it gets better. My therapist told me in my first session that it gets harder before it gets easier. It's something that's really hard to get past, but I'll be here for you if you need me."

Dee said, "Thank you."

The woman said, "Okay you're all set for Friday at four. Will that work for you?"

"Yes, that'll be fine."

"All right, the support group is down the hall. No need to sign in but maybe check with the leader to let her know it's your first time. There's usually super tasty cookies. We have a woman on staff who loves to bake, so you do not want to miss out on those."

They waved as they headed down the hall to the support group. Dee stopped in front of the door that had a sheet of white paper with *Sexual Assault Support Group* written in black marker attached with a piece of masking tape. A faint scent of chocolate chip cookies emitted from the room. They were definitely in the right place. Dee glanced back at Selena and she returned an encouraging nod.

Heart pounding, they entered a room that had fifteen orange plastic chairs arranged in a circle in the middle. There was a folding table on the side wall that displayed a coffee carafe, tea kettle, an assortment of tea packets, and the freshly baked goods. There were a few other female students already seated in the chairs fiddling with their phones.

An older woman with graying hair and a pair of spectacles attached to colorful beaded chains greeted them at the door. "Hello, I'm Rhonda."

Selena and Dee introduced themselves and Rhonda continued, "We're glad to have you. Please know you're free to share as much as you'd like or as little as you like. Some women like to share their story or something they're currently struggling with, or maybe even share a win for the week. If you'd like to take a seat, we'll start in a few minutes. We usually save the cookies for after the session. My goodness, they smell amazing. I'm gonna have to use all my will power to resist sneaking a nibble!"

Dee and Selena thanked her and found a seat within the circle. The chairs filled quickly. All but two were occupied by other victims. Those two chairs remained empty, presumably for the next two unfortunate women who would need them. Dee felt herself frowning. How could there be this many sexual assault victims in one place? Why was this so common?

Dee listened intently as the other young women shared their struggles and their victories. There were definitely common themes: fearful of everyday activities that they didn't fear before, difficulty sleeping, feelings of shame, afraid to trust new people.

The lone victory story was of one girl going on a first date since her attack. It was Selena's turn next. Anxiety washed over Dee, knowing she may have to introduce herself, and reveal that she was attacked, to the whole group.

Dee turned to her right to watch Selena as she began to share.

Selena picked at her fingernails as they lay in her lap. "I'm Selena."

The room whispered variations of hello.

She continued. "I was assaulted almost a year ago. I've made a lot of progress since then. I've learned self-defense and always carry my baton—I call her Bessie. She's in my pocket here." Selena patted her pocket. "I don't have the same fears I used to, but I'm always on alert. One thing I'm currently struggling with is for the first time since the incident, I have a crush on a guy. And he likes me, and he told me. But I told him I couldn't date him right now. Up until this guy, I didn't think I'd have romantic thoughts about anyone, ever again. Now I do. It makes me anxious, but I really like him. I've decided to talk to my therapist about it because I do want to go out with him, I'm just not sure I'm ready."

There were a lot of nods from the other women. Dee had no idea Selena was going through this. Was it Brendon that she was in to? She would ask her about it later.

Rhonda said, "Thank you for sharing, Selena, and we're glad to have you with us. I think a lot of these feelings are very common and I think you taking the next step to talk to your therapist about this man is a wonderful bit of progress for you. I wish you luck. Is there anyone else who'd like to share or maybe just introduce yourself?" She directed her eyes at Dee.

Dee's stomach churned. *Now or never.* "Hi, my name is Dee."

The same muted hellos and welcomes for Selena were now directed at Dee. She continued after it died down. "I was assaulted at the Delta Kappa Alpha house ten days ago. I haven't gone to class since the attack. It's really thrown me through a loop. The police don't want to press charges. They say that it's he said, she said, even though I did all the things I was supposed to do. It's really frustrating and I feel really angry. This is my first support group and I have my first counseling appointment on Friday."

Women around the circle shook their heads at her story. One woman from across the circle, with red hair and a spattering of freckles said, "Same thing happened to me, at the DKA house, I mean. Sorry to hear that, but I'm glad you're here. I'm still angry too, and it's been over a year for me."

The woman sitting next to the redhead turned her attention to Dee, in shock. "You got assaulted at Delta Kappa Alpha too?"

Dee's mouth dropped open, staring at these women as they exchanged their stories of being assaulted at the Delta Kappa Alpha house. By her count, five out of the twelve women in the room commiserated over being attacked at the DKA house. How could it be that it kept happening? At the same place? How had they not made the connection earlier?

Dee blurted out. "Do you know the name of your attacker?"

A few shook their hands sadly. One other said, "The bastard's name was Bill."

Another said, "Jake."

Dee couldn't believe what she was hearing. "Did your attacker get arrested?"

The red head said, "Nope. He said, she said."

The room erupted in chatter and similar stories.

Rhonda tried to get the crowd under control. "Okay, ladies. Let's settle down. We have only a few minutes left. Dee, thank you for sharing and welcome. Does anybody else have anything they'd like to share before we close out today's session?"

The women went silent.

Rhonda removed her glasses, letting them dangle on the multi-color beads. "Okay then. Thank you everyone for coming. I look forward to seeing you again next week. I'm sure none of you will forget to have some cookies and a warm beverage before you go. Be well."

Selena and Dee made their way over to the cookies. Selena turned to her and said, "Can you believe that there were five women who said they were assaulted at a DKA party? I wonder if we could put a case together, bring it to the police. Something should be done about this."

"What could we possibly do? It wasn't the same guy every time. And you heard what Detective Grayson said. He said, she said."

Selena had a fierce look in her eyes. "I don't know, but I think maybe there's something we could do to stop them—once and for all. The next group session isn't until after Thanksgiving break, but maybe we can come up with a plan and then present it to the support group?"

Dee didn't think she had the energy for a crusade. She said, "I don't know." There was one thing she was sure of, and that was that she would avoid the Delta Kappa Alpha house for the rest of her life and warn any other woman to do the same.

11

Sunday morning a week and a half later, Selena glanced up from her laptop at the sound of the door opening. "Dee?"

A voice called out. "It's me."

Selena shut the lid and hopped off her bed. She greeted Dee with a hug before they plopped themselves down on the sofa. "How was Thanksgiving?"

Dee shrugged. "It was fine. I didn't tell my family. It was kind of tricky to pretend like I'm loving school. Oh, well. It's kind of nice to be back in the dorm so I don't have to fake it so much. How was your Thanksgiving?"

Selena nodded. "It was good. It was nice to be home with Dad, Martina, and Zoey. My dad's a great cook. I think I ate my body weight in mashed potatoes and pumpkin pie. It was fun, but I'm glad to be back too." She also had a good strategy session with Martina about how to get evidence against the predators at DKA and, hopefully, get the fraternity shut down. Well, when they discussed it, it had been all hypothetical, but Selena sensed Martina knew she was up to something based on Martina's over-stating of all the dangers one could face and all the precautions one should take. Selena felt up to the challenge. There was no way it was coincidence all of those women had been assaulted at the same frat house. She would get to the bottom of it, not only to get justice for Dee and the others, but to prevent other women from falling prey to them.

"I bet. Have you run into any one special since you've been back?" Dee wiggled her eyebrows.

Selena scrunched up her face. "Not yet. I was going to head down there a little later and talk to him."

Dee's eyes opened wide, and she swallowed. "What are you going to say? Do you really think you're ready?"

She'd discussed Brendon with her therapist last week, and they agreed she was ready to go on a date. It excited her but terrified her at the same time. She'd grown to really care for Brendon, but that was what scared her most of all. "Something like, 'I like you and I want to go on a date with you.' Is that lame?" It was true, she did like him and wanted to go on a date with him, but she also needed him to escort her to a DKA party so she could initiate surveillance. Two birds, one stone.

Dee beamed at her. "It's direct. It's perfect. He'd be a fool to turn you down."

"Thanks." Selena could feel the swarm of butterflies already.

Selena stood in front of Brendon's door and took a deep breath. And another. And another. *C'mon, Selena, you can do this.* She raised her hand to knock and the door swung open. Brendon appeared wearing nothing but a pair of dark wash denim and a bright smile. *Damn.* He was fit. Selena's heart thudded in her chest and she momentarily forgot how to use her words.

"Hi, Selena, this is a nice surprise."

Words escaped her, and she blurted, "Hi." *Oh jeez, girl, you sound like an idiot.* It was not her finest moment.

He cocked his head with a knowing smile. "Did you want to come in?"

"Yeah, I was thinking if you have a few minutes, maybe we could talk?" It was so much harder than she'd practiced. Was it his shirtless body or his killer smile? He made her far more flustered than she was comfortable with.

"Come on in."

She could do this. She could. She walked to the living room and sat on the sofa. He continued to the bedroom and hollered out, "I'm gonna throw a shirt on, I'll be right back."

Thank goodness. She didn't think she could pull off the mission with him shirtless. He needed a shirt. She hadn't anticipated him without a shirt. Here Selena had thought she would never have feelings for another man again, now she could barely speak at the sight of a six pack. He returned and sat next to her on the sofa. "Okay, so what's this about?"

She turned to look at him, her breath caught once again. Oh boy. She really liked this guy. But she had to be smart. "I wanted to apologize for the last time I was over. It's been a long time since I've dated anyone, and the last breakup didn't go very well. It left me a little trigger shy." *Understatement of the century.*

"So, what you're saying is you've been hurt before and that's why you don't want to date me?"

"But the thing is, I do like you, and I thought maybe if you're okay with taking things slow, then maybe we could go out?" She stared at him as her heart raced.

A crooked smile crept up the side of his face. "I would very much like to go on a date with you. When would you like to go out?"

"How about Friday?" That way they could go out on a real date before she subtly suggested the two of them attend a Delta Kappa Alpha party.

He nodded. "I'm free on Friday. How about I pick you up at your dorm room and we can go to dinner?"

"Okay, great. Sounds good." She was about to push off the couch and leave when he stopped her by putting his hand gently on her arm. Her cheeks flushed.

"Do you have to leave right now?"

She really did not plan this as well as she thought she did. "No. Not really."

His eyes sparkled. "Do you want to hang out for a little bit?"

Was she really ready for this? She had her baton. "I can hang out for a bit."

"Great. Uh, do you want to watch a movie or ..." His eyes locked on hers, and he leaned toward her, placing his hand on her thigh. She didn't push him away. He continued until his lips met hers. The warmth of his mouth on hers sent heat down her body. It had been so long since she'd kissed someone, she had forgotten how wonderfully intoxicating it could be. She didn't want to stop. She kissed him back, wrapping her arms around his neck, feeling his hair with her fingers.

Fifteen minutes later, she was about ready to rip off his shirt and return him to his topless state when she froze. It was too much too fast. She had to stop. She pushed him back gently. Out of breath, she said, "I think I should go."

His eyes pleaded with hers. "Are you sure?"

She was sure. She leaned over to give him a warm soft kiss and then lifted herself off the sofa. "I'll see you on Friday." She hurried out of his dorm and prayed her need for a swift departure was due to nerves—and not echoes of her ex-boyfriend, Zeek, warning her to stay away.

12

Selena blotted her red lips with a tissue and then tossed the item into the trash. She flipped her head over and swung it back to give her long, wavy brown hair some body. Staring at her reflection, she still couldn't believe she was going on her first date since—well, since she thought she would never go on another date again. And then there was Brendon. The guy that made her tingly all over. She wanted to be with him, but she also needed to put an end to Delta Kappa Alpha's violence against women. She needed Brendon to help her, but she wasn't ready to let him in on her investigative plans. She only hoped that he wouldn't be mad if he ever found out. A tinge of guilt sparked inside of her. She kept telling herself she wasn't using him—because she wasn't, not really.

A knock on the door shook her out of her thoughts. Dee called out, "I'm pretty sure that's for you."

Selena exited the bathroom and eyed her roommate, who was sitting upright on her bed zoned in on the screen of her laptop. She was glad Dee had finally decided to go back to class and focus on her studies. Lucky for Dee, and thanks to her counselor, her professors had let her make up what she'd missed.

"I suppose it is. Don't wait up."

Dee chuckled. "As if I ever go to sleep."

It was sad, but true. She could hear her roommate tossing and turning all night. Her heart broke for Dee, but she knew that it would get better eventually. Selena herself wasn't a great sleeper, but compared to Dee she was practically a bear during hibernation season.

Selena waved and hurried toward the door, with butterflies in tow. She grabbed the handle, turned, and pulled. An involuntary smile took over at the sight of Brendon's sparkling light brown eyes and nervous grin.

"Hi."

"Hi. You look beautiful."

"Thanks." Her body went rigid as a flashback of Zeek infiltrated her thoughts. She liked compliments, but Zeek had love bombed her hard. Constant compliments and a steady stream of texts day and night. At the time, she'd thought it was flattering and sweet. She didn't realize it was just the early steps of what they call coercive control. She knew better now but, unfortunately, she'd had to learn the hard way. For her, compliments were complicated. She stepped over the threshold and shut the door behind her. She turned around to face him. "All set. Are you ready?"

"Yes, I thought we'd go to an Italian place. Do you like Italian food?"

"I love Italian. I'm Italian, you know." She said with a coy smile.

"No, I didn't know that. You don't have a very Italian last name."

"My mother's Italian. My dad isn't." Her mother *had been* Italian.

"That makes sense."

They made small talk as they exited the dorm and entered the parking structure where he had parked his car. Conversation was easy and casual as they drove into downtown San Francisco.

After finally finding a parking spot, Brendon parked and ran over to open the door for her. A year ago, she would've thought he was a gentleman. Now she wondered if he was a misogynist who wanted to keep her barefoot and pregnant. *I swear, you date one homicidal maniac and it changes your perspective on everything.*

She stepped out of the car, forcing a smile. "Thank you." Her nerves rattled as they walked down the sidewalk passing groups of people out for a good time. He opened the door to the restaurant and held it for her. She gave another apprehensive smile at the chivalrous gesture. She stepped in and immediately went up to the podium to put in their name. He came up behind her and said, "Oh, I have a reservation."

So much for trying to show that she didn't need him to lead the entire evening. She knew she was being overly sensitive, but that was her reality now.

The hostess sat them at a small table in the packed restaurant with twinkle lights above the bar that was situated in the middle of the restaurant. The hostess handed them large hardbound menus. *Fancy.* It was sweet that he had gone to the trouble. He peeked over the menu and said, "I'm glad I made a reservation, I just heard someone say that there was an hour wait. Also, they supposedly have the best gnocchi in town. Do you like gnocchi? It's one of my favorites."

He seemed so sweet and sincere. "I love all pasta, especially fettuccine."

"Me too. Looks like they have a pesto fettuccine."

Selena's stomach grumbled at the thought. "Yum."

After devouring the bread and olive oil dipping sauce, their entrées were presented to them on large white plates. Selena stared down at her order of half gnocchi and half pesto fettuccine. It smelled A.Maze.Ing. She couldn't wait to dig in. She glanced up at Brendon and met his gaze.

His eyes shined into hers. "Bon appétit."

"Bon appétit." She grabbed her fork and took a bite of the pesto fettuccine. She chewed with her mouth closed but couldn't help but moan. It was so good. Realizing she was making a spectacle of herself she looked over at Brendon, who had a wide smile.

Her cheeks burned. She obviously had lost the ability to act civilized on a date. Mouth still full of fettuccine, she mumbled, "Sorry. It's so good."

"Oh no, please don't apologize. I'm very much enjoying the show."

She swallowed. "Thanks. I feel so stupid now."

"Oh, no, no, don't feel silly. Here. This will make you feel better." He picked up his fork, stabbed a plump gnocchi, and popped it in his mouth. He began to chew and then he rubbed his belly in circles and started moaning rather loudly.

Selena almost fell over in laughter. "Stop that or they'll kick us out!"

"Feel better?" he asked.

A smile crept up her face. "Yes." He was sweet and silly and funny. It was as if he wasn't so much trying to impress her as he was trying to be a good date. She liked it and was enjoying every minute of their time together.

After they finished off their Spumoni and tiramisu, they exited the restaurant and stepped out onto the sidewalk. Brendon gently placed his hand in hers. She didn't pull away. She liked the warmth of his soft fingers. The strength of his hands.

When they approach the car, he turned her around to face

him. He looked down at her. "I'm having a great time tonight. Is it dorky if I ask you if you'll go out with me again?"

Yes, it was kind of dorky, but it was welcome too. Everything seemed so easy with him, it was almost effortless. "I had a good time too. So, yes, I'd go out with you again."

He smiled and bent down and kissed her softly. He stood back up and unlocked the door and opened it for her. She slid into the passenger seat and untangled her hand from his. He shut the door and headed over to the driver side. He seemed normal. She didn't feel afraid of him. That was a good sign, right?

They continued to chatter on the way back to their dorms. They talked about their classes and the upcoming holidays. Throughout the night he'd made her laugh so hard she thought she'd crack a rib.

As they walked back to their building, she secretly prayed that it wasn't a façade, that this was who Brendon really was. They held hands as they made their way back up to the third floor. They stopped at her door and Selena hesitated. She didn't want the night to be over, but she didn't want to invite him in with Dee inside. He must have sensed her hesitation. He said, "Did you want to turn in for the night, or maybe hang out at my place? My roommate went home for the weekend."

Selena looked up at him. "I'd like that."

A few hours later, Selena entered her dorm. As expected, Dee was still up, exactly where she had been when Selena left. Dee peered above the screen of the laptop and smiled. "Someone had a late night."

Selena kicked off her heels and sat crossed legged on her bed. "We decided to hang out after dinner."

"Hang out? Is that code for getting down?"

Selena could feel her face turning bright red.

"Dang, girl! Now I really want the details."

"We went to dinner downtown, it was amazing. The food was so good. And then we hung out his dorm room for a little bit."

"Hang out in his dorm for a little bit? Girl, it's almost two in the morning," Dee said with innuendo in her voice, looking at the time on her phone.

Yes, it was. She hadn't planned to be over his place for that long, but she had a hard time tearing herself away from him. "Nothing too salacious to report back."

"Really?"

"Just over-the-clothes stuff. I told him I wanted to take it slow."

Dee's expression turned serious. "So how was it, your first date since—everything?"

"It was good. It was fun and he makes me laugh. It was nice."

"I'm glad you had a nice night."

"Me too."

Was it possible she could actually have a relationship with Brendon? She certainly wasn't ready for anything more than the physical stuff they had done that night. He was understanding, but she could tell that he was having a difficult time. Her therapist had told her that only time would tell what she would be ready for and when.

She looked back at Dee and remembered her mission. She should be able to easily persuade Brendon to take her to the Delta Kappa Alpha house. She felt a tiny bit guilty not telling him her intentions, but she really did like him. So she wasn't deceiving him—not really. Even if she didn't need to get into the DKA house, she would still want to go on another date with him. So, it wasn't wrong, right?

13

Hand-in-hand, Brendon and Selena made their way up the steps to the massive, two-story Delta Kappa Alpha house. Music was blaring and dozens were milling about with drinks in hand. A typical Saturday night at a frat house.

Earlier in the week, Selena had suggested to Brendon that they go to the DKA house for a party. He'd agreed without any kind of hesitation or wondering why she wanted to go. She hadn't needed to give the excuse she'd prepared. She'd planned to say she'd never been to a frat party before and wanted to see what it was like. She was glad she hadn't had to lie because truth be told, she could have gone her entire life without visiting a fraternity—especially one known for assaulting women.

She and Brendon had seen each other a few times over the last week. Her feelings increased the more time they spent together. He didn't compliment her constantly or text her non-stop. She didn't think he was a Zeek 2.0. However, she'd asked her therapist for an opinion, still not fully trusting her own instincts. Her therapist listened as she described the date and Brendon. Her therapist had said that so far Brendon didn't seem to exhibit any red flags, but that she couldn't be sure because she hadn't met him in person. Selena wished Martina could give him the once-over. She'd be able to assess him no problem, but it was far too early for her to be introducing Brendon to her parents.

Brendon gave the bouncer their name. The burly man in a black t-shirt scanned a list and then said, "Alrighty, you're good to go."

"Thanks."

He led Selena into the house. It was loud, and people were dancing and drinking. It was as if the house was pulsating with its own life force. Each room was jam-packed with people clutching plastic cups. The air smelled of marijuana and cigarettes. Clearly an *anything goes* kinda place.

Brendon leaned over to speak directly into her ear. "Is this what you thought it would be like?"

She looked up at him. "It's a lot louder and with a lot more people than I would've thought." Easy to get lost in the crowd and lose the person you'd come with.

"Yeah, it can get pretty crazy, but it can be fun too. Do you like to dance?"

"Sure." She couldn't remember last time she'd danced.

"Well, come on." He led her into one of the main rooms that was loosely being used as a dance floor.

They flailed about, dancing their hearts out to a Lady Gaga tune. Brendon was a terrible dancer. Selena wasn't much better. They giggled as he twirled her around in a faux dramatic dance move. They danced until they were sweaty and laughing so hard they had to get off the dance floor to catch their breath.

Leaned up against a wall covered with striped wallpaper, Brendon gazed down at her. "I have the best time with you. I really lucked out that you were assigned to my floor."

"Me too."

He gave her a light kiss and then stepped back. "Have you seen enough? You wanna get out of here?"

She hadn't planted the cameras yet. Shoot! She had nearly forgotten the entire reason for coming here. "Yeah, I, uh, just have to go to the bathroom first."

He gave her a bit of a strange look. "Can you wait until we get back? This place is a little sketch."

Things were a little sketch around here? How much did Brendon know about what went on at the frat? "It's okay. I'll be quick. I really need to go. I'll be right back." She patted him on the shoulder and ran off to find the bathroom. *Her first lie.* She shook off the guilt and told herself it was for a good cause.

She hurried down the hall and tried to blend in with the drunken partygoers. She made a quick right and hopped up to the top of the stairs. There was an outlet right in the center. She pulled out the USB charger, which was actually a secret camera, from her shoulder bag and quickly plugged it in. Next she made her way to the first open door. A bedroom with a king size bed, two nightstands, and a furry bean bag chair in the corner. She hesitated about planting another device. A bedroom seemed like a good place to record but also like a huge violation. Like maybe a jail-time kind of violation. No, she'd plant one in the living room and at an outside socket instead.

She turned around to leave and froze. She was face-to-face with Tyler. *Shit.* "What are you doing in here?" he asked.

Selena feigned innocence. "I was just looking for a bathroom. Can you help?" The excuse that literally everyone makes when they sneak around in someone else's house.

"The bathrooms for guests are downstairs. Wait, don't I know you?"

Selena's nerves rattled. "I don't think so. I'm, uh, Tina. You are?" *Be cool, Selena, be cool.*

A creepy smile lit up his face. "I'm Tyler. It looks like you need a drink. "

Um. No. "Oh yeah, actually, I'm here with a friend I should get back. Maybe later. Okay, bye." She didn't wait for a response. Instead, she rushed past him, down the hall, and down the stairs, hoping he wouldn't follow. The last thing she needed was for Tyler to find out what she was up to.

At the bottom of the stairs, Brendon stood with a puzzled look on his face. "What were you doing up there?"

Double shit. "Oh, I was hoping for a more private bathroom. It's okay now, we can go." She grabbed his hand and gave him a nervous smile. She'd have to plant the other cameras another day. *Shit.* This was not going according to plan.

She tried to lead him out, but he stopped. "What's going on, Selena? You're acting strange."

Think fast. "I just really have to go. I, uh, started my period." *Lie number two.* Now her nerves were officially shot, and she just wanted to go home.

Brendon's face turned a pale shade of pink. "Oh, okay. We can go."

Both relief and guilt flowed through her. She didn't like lying to him, even if it was for a good cause.

14

Selena approached the house and tugged her black knit beanie down almost to her eyebrows. It was a frigid night and her black turtleneck and hoodie with black jeans and black boots was appropriate attire, but skulking around in the dark *not so much*. She scanned the steps and porch of the Delta Kappa Alpha house. There wasn't anybody outside. Apparently, the only night they didn't party was on Mondays.

Coast clear, she tiptoed alongside the house. She paused and stared at the now dead grass. Was that where Dee was attacked? Is this where they attacked all their victims? She turned and kneeled down. Power outlet on the porch. Check. She pulled out a camera from the pouch on the front of her hoodie and plugged it in. A bit of an oddity if anyone noticed it, but she had to take the chance. She stood back up and scanned the perimeter. No one was around.

Hunched down, she continued on. She crept up to the first window and peeked in from the corner. It was the side living room where the dance floor had been located. Now there were just a few guys sitting on some sofas. Not assaulting anyone. *Good job, guys*. It was nobody she recognized. She kept on until she reached the kitchen window. She peeked inside, but there was nobody in the kitchen.

She ducked back down and crept along the wall until she reached the gate to the backyard. She stopped and listened. Silence. She slipped her arm over to undo the latch and pulled it open as quietly as she could. Her heart sped up as the creak of the hinges made far too much noise. If there was anybody out there, she would've been found out.

She kept her hand on the top and let it slowly close without relatching. She surveyed the backyard. There were several sets of low tables with matching chairs and a large fire pit in the center. She focused her attention to the right. There was a sliding glass door that led into the house. She shimmied along the wall to take a peek inside.

She leaned out to take a quick glimpse. There were three men standing in the corner, two she didn't recognize and one she did. It was only a side profile, but she would recognize that mustache anywhere. What the hell was Detective Grayson doing inside the Delta Kappa Alpha house?

He turned his head and she stepped back, hoping she wasn't visible. Adrenaline soared through her veins and her hands began to tremble. She needed to get out of there now. She walked backward until she hit the gate. She turned quickly and spotted another outlet. She pulled the second camera out and stuck it in. The slider began to open and she turned to make a run for it.

She made it to the front of the house, next to the porch, when she heard someone call out, "Hey!"

She instinctively turned to look. *Shit.* Tyler ran down the stops.

He was fast.

Now face-to-face, he asked, "What are you doing here?

"Oh, I thought I left something at the party last week and I was just looking for it." Dressed in head to toe black.

He gave her a devilish smirk. "Really? What exactly is it that you lost?"

Not buying it. C'mon, Selena, try harder. "My bracelet. It's gold and has a little dangling heart on it. Have you seen it?" She knew she wasn't being believable, but she needed to get the hell out of there. She'd now technically met Tyler three times. He could probably identify her. That was just dandy, but what she really needed was to ensure Detective Grayson didn't lay eyes on her— she needed to get away and fast. Detective Grayson would know something was up immediately if he saw her lurking around.

He said, "No. Sorry."

"Okay then, well I checked and didn't see it either. I must've lost it somewhere else. Thanks anyways. Bye." She tried to casually stroll off, but he grabbed her by the arm, swinging her back around.

"Not so fast. I remember you. I found you in one of the bedrooms. Tina? Maybe you and I should get more acquainted."

Oh, hell no. "I really have to go."

He squeezed her arm harder. "No, I don't think that's true. I think you should come inside with me."

She was certainly not going inside the house with a rapist. She put her hand in the pouch of her hoodie, hand on baton, ready for action. "No, I won't be doing that. I'm going to go."

His hands were stronger than she expected. He wasn't letting her go. She looked him dead in the eyes. "Let go of my arm or mark my words, you will regret it."

"What are you gonna do, little girl?"

She pulled the baton out of the pouch and flicked it to full length, rotated her arm, and whacked him on the wrist. He immediately let go and cried out in pain. He shouted, "You bitch!"

She sprinted at top speed until she reached the Towers. Fighting in real life was not at all like she'd practiced in the gym. In the gym, fear and rage hadn't been a factor. By the time she'd arrived at her dorm room, sweat trickled down her back and her hair was soaked beneath her beanie. The mission hadn't gone great, but she did manage to plant two more cameras. She took off the beanie and caught the elevator up to the third floor.

What the hell was Detective Grayson doing at the DKA house? Was he investigating? Did he know about the rapes at the house? Was he helping them cover it up? Was he in on it? He acted like he hadn't known Tyler when Dee had shown him his photo, but that couldn't have been the case. What the hell had she stumbled upon?

15

Out of breath, Selena slammed the door and engaged the deadbolt before rushing over to her bed and popping open the lid to her laptop. From across the room, she heard, "How did it go?"

Selena continued working on the laptop without looking over at Dee. "They're installed, but I didn't get away undetected. I ran into Tyler. He wouldn't let me go, so I hit him with my baton and ran as fast I could back here."

"Oh. My. God. Seriously?"

Selena said, "uh-huh" as she remained focused on the screen. "And you'll never believe this." She furiously tapped the keys of her laptop to access the camera she'd just installed. It opened up. There was nobody in the side yard. She moved to outdoor camera two in the backyard. Detective Grayson standing with the two men and now Tyler. She couldn't hear what they were saying, but she could tell that Grayson was questioning Tyler based on his hand gestures and the direction of his eyes. It appeared he was asking about Tyler's wrist, which he held with his other hand. She'd hit him as hard as she could. She wouldn't be surprised if she'd broken it.

Selena spotted Dee in the corner of her eye as she scampered over to Selena's bed to watch the screen. "Holy shit. Is that Detective Grayson?"

Selena turned to her. "Yep. He was inside the house when I got there. I hurried out because I saw him through the window heading toward the back patio. But when I jogged out, I ran into Tyler. Like I said, I hit him pretty hard."

Dee shook her head. "Why would Detective Grayson be there?"

"My friend, that is a very good question." She inched closer to the screen and watched as they headed back into the house. Thankfully, they hadn't been compelled to investigate why she'd been there in the first place. If they found the cameras, her efforts would be for nothing. Despite the small win, her nerves continued to rattle and she begun to wonder if she was in over her head.

Maybe she should confess her covert investigation to Martina and get some backup, but she knew Martina wouldn't be pleased by her actions.

She could wait. There were only four days left before winter break and the fraternity was throwing a big party before everybody went home to celebrate the holidays with their families. She would give it a little more time. She switched to the camera inside the house. Nothing unusual. Just the typical empty staircase and hallway. She could feel Dee staring at her. "What?" Selena asked.

"Nothing. It's just crazy that you were able to get video surveillance and be virtually undetected. It's cool and kinda scary. You don't have any cameras in here, do you?" Dee nudged her playfully.

Selena gave her a puzzled look. "Of course not. This is solely for the purpose of shutting down these assholes. I'm not some kinda creeper."

Dee chuckled. "If you say so."

Selena eyed Dee. She was glad Dee found a reason to smile, even if it was at her expense. She refocused and retrieved the saved footage from the Cloud to see if the interaction with Tyler had been recorded. Bingo. At least now she had a defense if Tyler tried to say he was attacked unprovoked, if he chose to report the incident. Hopefully, he knew better than to do something that stupid. She didn't exactly want to have to show footage that was obtained with her secret camera, but she would if it kept her out of jail.

With recording and saving verified, she was ready for the next party. She'd review footage between now and then as she had time, but she had a feeling she wouldn't get anything usable until the party on Thursday.

Then she'd stake out in front of her laptop. Luckily, all of her finals would be done by then. It would be her last chance before the break to catch them in the act and hopefully stop another attack and get them shut down for good.

Dee stood up and curled back up on her bed. "Why do you think the detective was there? I suppose he could be questioning them, but I really don't think so. Do you think he's covering up the assaults for them? But why would he do that?"

Selena mused. It would be a bonus to understand why Detective Grayson was at the fraternity in the first place. He was clearly friendly with the fraternity brothers in the house.

Dee interrupted her thoughts. "Do you know how to do background checks and search for any connections?"

Not a bad idea. Selena shook her head. "Not without the team at work knowing about it. But maybe they would be okay with it if I explained that it was to see if he had a reason to drop all of the cases. I don't have to say because I saw him at the frat. I should be able to do it without raising any suspicions that I'm running my own investigation. That's a great idea, Dee."

Dee chortled. "I have my moments."

Her nerves were calming now. It was empowering to be able to take action against these people, instead of just waiting for the next victim to show up in their support group. She wondered what she would find in Detective Grayson's background.

She looked across at Dee. "Yes, you do. Yeah, I'll do the background tomorrow when I get into the office. We still have a few days before the big party."

Selena's back pocket buzzed. She slipped the phone out and stared at the screen. It was Brendon. Had he seen her running down the hallway?

She answered it. "Hi, Brendon," she said and used hand signals to let Dee know that she was going to take the call in the living room.

Selena curled up on the sofa.

"Hi, I was just calling to see how you're doing and wanted to know if you maybe want to go out and get a bite to eat?"

What if she ran into Tyler when she was out with Brendon? She needed to lay low until after the big party on Thursday night. Maybe they could stay in. "Would you want to order a pizza and maybe hang out instead?"

"Sure."

"Is your roommate home?"

"Nope. He just went to a study group thing. You want to come over here?"

"Okay."

"I'll order the pizza. What do you like on your pizza?"

Selena said, "Mushrooms, olives, and maybe sausage?"

"Sounds great. I'll call right after I get off the phone with you. When can you be over?"

Selena scanned down her body. She was sticky from dried

sweat. She'd need a shower and primping time before she went over to Brendon's. "Give me thirty minutes."

"Okay, see you then."

"Bye." She pressed end and set the phone face down on the sofa. She was excited to see him, but she needed to keep her head on straight. She'd had a win tonight, but also a setback; Tyler had remembered her fake name, but not her real name from their actual first meeting. She had to be careful to not run into him again before the party. And then, hopefully, all of this would be over. She wouldn't have to worry about Tyler or having to lie to Brendon anymore. She *really* hated lying to him.

16

Selena glanced down at her phone and read Brendon's latest text: ARE YOU SURE YOU CAN'T TAKE A LITTLE STUDY BREAK? She sat at the dining table, watching the cameras at the DKA house. It was nearly 11 o'clock on Thursday night, and so far nothing illegal had happened other than what was likely underaged drinking. Brendon had wanted to hang out since both of them were going home to see their families the next day.

I'M TOTALLY SWAMPED, LAST MINUTE STUDYING FOR THE TAKE-HOME FINAL. MAYBE LATER. TALK SOON.

Lie number three. Dishonesty wasn't a great way to start out their relationship, especially since she really liked him.

Was jeopardizing her relationship with Brendon worth shutting down the Delta Kappa Alpha house? Yes. This wasn't just for her or for Dee, this was for all the women who could be spared a brutal attack. This was bigger than herself. But she didn't exactly like the idea of having to make a choice if it came up. She'd hoped she'd be able to keep her relationship with Brendon intact *and* take down the frat. Fingers crossed.

OKAY. TTYL.

She replied with an emoji blowing him a kiss.

Her focus returned to the screen. People were parting it up in the backyard smoking cigarettes and other smokable devices.

She now understood why Martina insisted patience was valuable in this line of work. She been watching the cameras for two hours and she was on her fourth cup of coffee. It was her first stakeout and, so far, it was pretty damn boring. She didn't even have Dee to keep her company.

Dee had decided to go home early since her finals were finished. Selena encouraged it but now wished she'd had some company. If she weren't on a stakeout, it would've been a great opportunity to have Brendon over so they could have their own celebration before they went home for the holidays. But she had priorities and she had to think of more than just herself and Brendon. She personally knew five women who were assaulted at that fraternity house and at a minimum she wanted to shut it down, kind of like a Christmas gift to the women of SFU.

The background check had come back for Detective Grayson, San Francisco University alumni and member of Delta Kappa Alpha. *Go figure.* Apparently, once a DKA brother, you're a DKA brother for life. It was clear to her that he was protecting DKA because they were his fraternity brothers, despite the oath he took as a police officer to serve and protect. But was he in on the crimes or just covering them up?

The camera inside the house showed a very intoxicated woman going upstairs with one of the frat brothers. It made her stomach flip. She wanted to scream, "Don't go up there!" But it would've been useless. Selena now realized the hallway and staircase footage wasn't that useful other than if evidence was needed to corroborate that certain persons had gone upstairs. Hopefully, it didn't come to that. She had regretted installing the inside camera after taking a closer look at the laws around surveillance. If the authorities found out she'd placed cameras inside the house, she could get into a lot of trouble. It was one of the reasons she'd decided against bringing Martina into the operation. It would implicate her in these crimes, not to mention Selena was sure Martina would be disappointed. She convinced herself the cameras outside were in more of a gray area.

Two hours later, camera one, on the side of the house was triggered on. It was the first time all evening. On the screen appeared a woman wearing far too little for the temperature outside, and a tall, burly man with shoulder-length hair. Was the side yard the hotspot for these guys? The couple on the screen began to kiss rather aggressively. Selena felt a bit dirty watching two people make out when they didn't know they were being watched. But she supposed it was one of those things she'd have to get used to if she became a detective or private investigator. She still needed another year and a half at Drakos Monroe before she could apply for her PI license, if she decided that route over going into law enforcement. After watching Detective Grayson, she was leaning toward private investigator. She didn't think she could handle working for or with a crooked cop.

She continued to watch the gross make-out. Everything seemed to be on the up-and-up so far. The girl certainly wasn't fighting back. She had her fingers in his hair as if she was enjoying the action. She watched the man's hands as they slipped down the woman's body until he reached the hem of her mini dress. He slid it underneath and the woman batted at his hand in what looked like an attempt for him to remove his hand. It didn't appear to be working. He became more aggressive lifting up the dress, now fully exposing the bottom half of her body. The woman struggled against him while simultaneously trying to push down her dress.

Selena's heart raced as she dialed 9-1-1 on the burner phone she purchased for the occasion. "Hi, yes, I'm calling to report an assault outside the Delta Kappa Alpha house. Please come right away. It's still in progress." She hung up the line and returned her attention to the screen. She watched the woman continuing to try to fight off the man.

Selena's heart pounded and sweat trickled on her for head. There was no way the police would get there in time. What had she been thinking? She couldn't stand by and watch. She just couldn't. She laced up her Nikes, threw on her puffy jacket, and ran out of the dorm. As she sprinted across campus to the fraternity house, she now understood why Martina had pushed her to be in top physical condition.

Selena ran toward the fence line at the Delta Kappa Alpha house when she looked left and saw another figure speed-walking the same way. She recognized the mustache. *Detective Grayson.* She stopped in her tracks in an attempt to look a bit more inconspicuous in front of the plainclothes detective. Something in his eyes seemed to register that this wasn't her first time at the house. He sped toward her, pointing his finger. "It was you."

Selena reached for her baton, but before she could pull it out of her pocket, he had her pinned sideways against the fence, no more than twenty feet from where the woman was hopefully still fighting off her attacker. Inches from her face, Grayson spat at her. "What were you doing here Monday night?"

Selena wasn't sure how to play the situation. Should she fight back immediately or try to convince him that it wasn't her on Monday night? She struggled to free her arms. "I don't know what you're talking about. Let me go."

"Oh, I think you do, young lady. What were you doing here? I will only ask you nicely once. I'd hate to have to arrest you for trespassing."

"I don't know what you're talking about, and I'm not trespassing."

"It's my word against yours. He said, she said, but in this case he said is a detective with the police force. Who do you think they're going to believe, me or some little girl?"

Selena attempted to contort her body against the might of his two hands pressing her against the fence. He stared intently at her. "I'm watching you, Selena—or should I say Tina? Stay away from this house or you will regret it."

Her eyes locked on Detective Grayson's and she decided to give him three more seconds before she kneed him in the balls and then delivered a roundhouse kick to the face. He may know she possessed a baton, if he believed she was the person who had hit Tyler, but he wouldn't expect that she had the skills to take him down. The sound of multiple sets of footsteps seemed to prompt him to release her. She was about to run, when she eyed the source of the footsteps. Her heart sank. *Brendon. With Tyler.*

Brendon furrowed his brow. "Selena, what are you doing here?"

Standing next to him was Tyler, and his eyes widened. "Selena? I thought your name was Tina. She's the bitch that broke my wrist."

Selena couldn't look at Brendon. She knew she should run, but she also knew she couldn't run away from him forever.

"What? Is that true? Did you break his wrist? When? How? Why?" Brendon's eyes begged her for answers.

Detective Grayson said, "Tyler, is this the woman who assaulted you?"

Tyler rubbed the cast on his wrist. "Yep, that's her."

"Do you want to press charges?"

Selena stood staring at the three men with her hand firmly planted on her baton. The weapon in question. But she knew, and he didn't, that she had the whole interaction on video—not that she wanted it to go that far. It would blow her whole operation, not to mention maybe her relationship with Brendon.

Brendon cocked his head toward her. "Selena, what are they talking about? I thought you were at home studying."

She glanced over at him, looking defeated. "I'll explain everything later. I have to go. It was self-defense. He tried to do to me what he did to Dee."

His chin scrunched back to his neck. "What are you talking about? What happened to Dee?"

"Brendon, I'm sorry, I have to go."

Brendon stared at her dumbfounded.

She squeezed her eyes shut and then reopened them. "I have to go."

Tyler baited Detective Grayson. "You just gonna let her go?"

Detective Grayson glared at him. "I'm off duty. Let it go—for now."

She shook her head in disbelief before running back to the dorm, tears streaming down her cheeks.

17

Selena stood in her bathroom. Hands on thighs, bent over, heaving in and out as she tried to catch her breath. She had evidence, but she'd also been found out. Would they find her cameras too? She suddenly felt so very alone and wasn't sure what to do next. Her cell phone continued to buzz with calls and texts from Brendon. She hadn't answered. She couldn't. Who could she trust? She couldn't go to campus police, she knew that for sure. She could go to the San Francisco Police Department. The tiny sense of hope washed away. No, she knew who she needed to call.

Her breathing slowed. She turned on the sink faucet and splashed water on her face. She grabbed the towel and wiped off her face. She picked up her cell and dialed. Martina picked up on the first ring. "Is everything okay?"

"I need your help." She went on to explain to Martina everything that had happened with Dee, the support group, and the Delta Kappa Alpha house. Her investigation. The cameras. The evidence she had against the frat and that Detective Grayson was actually a member of the fraternity and was likely covering up the DKA assaults. After Selena described everything in detail, Martina simply said, "I'll be there in thirty minutes. Don't open the door for anyone but me."

Selena pulled the phone away from her ear and stared at the screen. Martina had ended the call.

She had feared Martina would give her a lecture, but she hadn't, at least not yet. The phone buzzed again. Another text from Brendon. WHY ARE AVOIDING MY CALLS?

Selena took a few breaths and tapped a message back. I CAN'T TALK RIGHT NOW. She put her phone down and let out one last good cry before stepping into the shower.

Fresh and clean, Selena sat at the dining table staring at the screen while waiting for Martina. At the sound of the knock at the door, Selena ran to the door. Rushing to open it, she almost forgotten to look through the peephole.

She stood back, opening it. Martina entered and shut the door quickly behind her. She put her arms around Selena in a warm, tight hug.

Martina studied Selena's face. "Are you okay?"

"I guess. I just feel stupid."

Martina raked her fingers through her short dark hair. "What you did was brave, but not necessarily the smartest thing to do, Selena. We'll talk about that later, but for now show me what you have. Can you do that?"

Selena nodded and brought Martina over to the dining table where she had her laptop open. She played back the footage, wincing at the sight of the woman's attack—the woman had not been able to stop the larger man, but it had been over before Selena even reached the house—and then her own episode with Detective Grayson. Martina sat back, hand covering her mouth. She placed it in her lap. "You say the older man with the mustache is a detective?"

"Yes, he's the one Dee and I went to, to report her assault. He's the one who said he talked to Tyler and Tyler said that Dee had initiated the whole thing and she wanted it and it was consensual."

"Do you know the other two guys that are there?"

"The one with the cast is Tyler. The other is ... Brendon. He's kind of my boyfriend. Well, we're dating. He didn't know about any of this stuff."

Martina's eyes were wide. "You're dating someone who hangs around with crooked cops and rapists?"

Selena shook her head. "No, he's not like that. At least, I don't think so. He's not in the frat. He told me he met Tyler during rush week. He said they're just friends, someone to hang out with, but he's how I got into the frat in the first place. That's how I was able to plant the first camera."

Martina went pale. "In the house?"

"In a hallway ... in the house."

Martina rested her forehead on her palm.

Not a good sign.

Martina sat up straight. "Selena, if the authorities find out about this, you could be in a lot of trouble. Do you realize that?"

"I do now. I just, I don't know what I was thinking. I just really want to get them shut down. I personally know five—now six—women who were assaulted there. There's likely tons more who were too afraid to report it."

Martina put her hand on her shoulder. "We'll get through this. It'll be okay. I promise."

Selena glanced up at Martina and wondered who she was trying to convince—herself or Selena. She knew she had disappointed Martina with her reckless actions, but she was grateful that her stepmom was still here for her and hopefully would help her take down the frat. "What do we do?"

"I still have contacts at the SFPD. We could bring them the footage of the outside—*not* any surveillance from the inside.

Maybe they'll be able to at least shut down the party tonight. I'll make some calls. The footage is in the Cloud?"

"Yes."

"Selena, this is what I'll say right now. You did fairly decent work here. It makes me think you'd be a great investigator, but what you did was far too dangerous. When we run an investigation, surveillance and stake outs, we have backup on call, we have people who always know where everyone else is supposed to be. It protects us in the case an operation goes sideways, but even then, it's dangerous. You were all by yourself, Selena. Please promise me you'll never do anything like this, ever again. It would break not only my heart but your dad's if something happened to you."

Selena felt tears welling up in her eyes once again. She never wanted to disappoint her dad or Martina. She blinked back the tears. "I promise."

"Okay, let me make some calls. Sit tight you and get ready to go with me to the station."

Selena nodded.

Selena watched as Martina took control of the situation. She'd been lucky to get out of this unharmed. She needed to be more careful next time.

A knock on the front door startled both Martina and Selena. Martina put a finger to her lips and motioned for Selena to stay seated. She slowly crept up to the door, hand on her gun holster. She peeked into the hole and then stepped back. She eyed Selena. "I think it's Brendon."

Selena lowered her eyes. She didn't want to see him or talk to him. She wasn't sure how to tell him what had happened. She didn't think he'd be very happy with her. Selena glanced back up at Martina and shook her head.

Martina gave a quick nod and she opened the door. "Hi, Brendon, my name is Martina."

"Oh, hi, is Selena here?"

"Selena is here, but she's not able to speak with you right now. I'm going to need for you to give her some space. She'll call you tomorrow when everything is settled."

"Is she okay?"

Martina glanced over her shoulder, back at Selena. "Selena's okay. I'm her stepmother. I'll have her give you a call tomorrow. Okay?"

"All right. You'll tell her I came by?"

Martina nodded before shutting the door. Martina glanced back at Selena. "You heard all that?"

Selena whispered, "Yeah."

"He seems nice."

"I think he is." *He is.* It was Selena who wasn't a very good girlfriend. Not that they'd had the relationship talk. Now they may never.

Martina gave her a sheepish grin. "You ready?"

"I'm ready."

She was ready—to shut Delta Kappa Alpha down.

Selena followed Martina into the San Francisco Police Department headquarters. Martina strutted up to reception. "I'm here to see Lieutenant Tippin."

"And who may I tell him is here?"

"Martina Monroe. I called earlier, he's expecting me."

"All right, I'll let him know you're here. You can take a seat."

"Thank you."

Seated in the chairs, Martina turned and faced Selena. "Tippin and I go way back. I'm hoping he will go to the frat tonight and at a minimum close down the party. He should be able to prosecute the man who attacked the woman, if we can identify them both. As for Grayson, it may be a bit tricky. In the video, he is clearly assaulting you, but he's also in law enforcement, so I'm not so sure. And one other thing: I will answer all the questions in there. You don't say a peep. It's for your own protection."

"What if he asks me a direct question?"

"I will answer for you. You told me everything, absolutely everything?"

"Yes." It had been a long ride down to the police station. Martina didn't scold her beyond her initial concerns, but her body language told Selena everything.

It was only a minute or two before the detective walked out. He approached, wide smile on his face. "Martina Monroe, great to see you. This must be Selena."

Martina spoke for her. "Yes, this is my stepdaughter, Selena Bailey. She is a student at San Francisco University."

"Okay, great, why don't you both follow me back."

Selena did as she was told, but the walk back to the detective's office gave her a sinking feeling, just as it had the first time she had gone down to the police department in Grapton Hill after her mother's death. She wondered if she'd ever escape those awful memories. The police department didn't look much different than the one in Grapton Hill. A bunch of cubicles and offices, people working and looking busy at their computers.

It was nice to be on the other side, this time. *Not a victim.*

Lieutenant Tippin opened the door to his office and sat himself behind the large desk. Martina and Selena sat across from him in two plastic office chairs. Lieutenant Tippin said, "Based on our phone conversation, it sounds like you've got a fraternity down at SFU that is known for assaulting women and getting away with it. You say campus police may be covering it up?"

Selena was about to speak when Martina put her hand on

Selena's arm. Martina said, "Yes. My stepdaughter is in a sexual assault support group where nearly half of the women in that support group were raped at the Delta Kappa Alpha house. One being my stepdaughter's roommate. All of the young woman had reported incidents, but all were told they couldn't be prosecuted because of the whole he said, she said thing and that the members of the frat claimed that all of their encounters had been consensual. There is one detective who was handling all of these investigations, Detective Grayson. Who we now know was actually a member of the Delta Kappa Alpha fraternity. We have obtained some video surveillance showing an assault on a young woman by one of the frat house members as well as an assault on my stepdaughter by Detective Grayson."

Lieutenant Tippin sat back in his chair and rubbed his shiny, bald head. He studied Selena and then Martina.

Martina spoke. "You watched the videos that I sent you?"

"I have. We'll need to identify the victim in the video as well as the perpetrator. And, Selena, I'll need you to explain what happened in the altercation between you and Detective Grayson where he is holding you up against the fence."

Martina leaned forward. "Tippin, for now I'm going to speak for Selena. She has explained to me everything that's happened. What she's told me is that she was there because she had been made aware of the assault on the woman and she wanted to go and try to stop it. Before she could reach the young woman, she was accosted by Detective Grayson. As you can see in the video. And you can also see it's likely the only reason he let her go was that two other people approached. One of the men is actually dating Selena and the other one is the person who attacked her roommate."

Lieutenant Tippin eyed Selena again. "Martina, if we didn't go as far back as we do, I'd be hesitant to act. But since I know you, I know you wouldn't have brought this to me if you didn't think we could make a case,—which based on the video we can, if it's not thrown out due to the nature of how it was obtained. Either way, I went ahead and began assembling a team to go out to the fraternity tonight. They are en route as we speak. Hopefully, we'll catch the perp and get a chance to question Detective Grayson. For now, we're playing this as an anonymous tip. At a minimum, a visit by the police will usually shut down the party. There is no question underaged drinking is going on—there always is. We don't usually get involved with university matters, but because of our *anonymous tip* that campus police is covering up illegal activity, we'll go in. I think it's best that both of you go back to the dorm, pack up your things, and go home. And for the love of all that is holy, *stay away* from the Delta Kappa Alpha house. Not just tonight, but in the future too."

Martina tipped her chin. "Noted." She turned to Selena. "You're done with your finals, right, Selena?"

Selena nodded and a spark of energy ignited within her. If Lieutenant Tippin's team was successful, it would have all been worth it.

"All right, ladies, well, I'm gonna get to it. Martina, don't be a stranger. Selena, pleasure to meet you. I'll keep you posted."

Martina grinned. "Thanks, Tippin. I owe you one."

"Yes, you do." He gave her a wink and shook Martina's hand before showing them the door.

18

Despite Lieutenant Tippin's suggestion to get out of town early that morning, Selena decided to get some sleep before hitting the road. Martina had offered to stay with her in case she wanted extra security, but Selena told her she'd be fine. And yet, Martina had insisted, commandeering the sofa in the living room. Selena knew better than to argue.

After a fitful five hours of sleep and a nice hot shower, Selena finished stuffing her suitcase with all the clothes and items she'd need over winter break. She pressed down on the carryon with all her weight as she forced it to zip shut. She lifted the suitcase from the bed and dropped it on the floor with a thud.

From the living room, Martina called out, "All packed?"

"Yep." She rolled the suitcase into the living room, where she sat on the couch with her cell phone in hand.

"What time is he coming over?" Martina asked.

"In about twenty minutes."

"Do you want me to ... Oh hold on."

Selena strolled over to the fridge while Martina took a call in the other room. She pulled out the last container of strawberry yogurt and grabbed a spoon from the drawer before sitting herself down at the table. Despite her nerves, her stomach was growling for sustenance. As she ate, she contemplated how she'd now finished her first semester at college and conducted her first unofficial investigation. Now, if she could not lose her first not-a-psycho-boyfriend, that would be *great*.

Selena tossed the container in the recycling and rinsed the spoon in the sink. The closer it grew to Brendon's arrival, the more jittered her nerves became.

"Good news!"

Selena swiveled around. "Yeah?"

"I just got off the phone with Lieutenant Tippin. They arrested the attacker in the video, but Detective Grayson wasn't at the frat when Tippin's team arrived. He's not sure an inquiry into Grayson will go anywhere—being in law enforcement and all—but the young man who sexually assaulted the woman is in jail and she's at a local hospital. You couldn't see on the camera, but she was lying on the ground farther back on the side of the house. Apparently, she has a heart condition. If the police hadn't found her when they busted the party, she may have died."

"Oh my god."

"Selena, that's because of you. We still need to discuss your methods ... but you saved a young woman's life. You should be proud. Also, because of the incident, it's likely the fraternity will lose its charter and get shut down."

"That's great!" Selena couldn't believe it. Her operation had paid off, in large part to Martina and her connections at the SFPD, but still. It made her realize that her path toward investigations was the right one for her. If felt amazing to be able to help that woman. She only wished she'd been able to get there before she'd been attacked. At least there was now one less predator on the streets.

A knock on her door made her heart nearly jump out of her chest.

Martina said, "I'll take your stuff down to the car and give you two a little privacy."

"Thanks."

Martina grabbed the handle of Selena's carry on suitcase and strolled over to the door. She let Brendon in on her way out, mouthing *good luck* to Selena as she shut the door behind her.

Selena forced a smile at him. "Hi."

"Hey."

She stood frozen. "You wanna sit?"

"Sure."

Selena sat stiffly on the sofa. Brendon sat on the other end. There were no smiles. No shining eyes.

Time to be brave. "How are you?"

Brendon met her gaze. "I'm okay. Confused. What are all these things I'm hearing?"

"What are you hearing?"

"Tyler says you attacked him. You were sneaking around the frat when you said you were studying. You lied to me."

Selena couldn't argue with that. She had lied to him. He just didn't realize how many times. She knew now was the time to come clean with him and to be completely honest. If they were to continue dating, she figured she owed him that much. Although, she knew this may be the end for the two of them. The truth didn't make her sound great.

"I'll explain everything." She went on to tell him the whole story about Dee, Tyler, running into him in the hall, the other women in her support group, her stakeout, and the current status of the case based on Tippin's latest update.

His cheeks were red. Was that anger in his eyes? "You used me to get into the frat house and obtain evidence against Tyler and the other frat brothers, who you assumed were assaulting women at the frat?"

"I didn't 'use' you. I mean, I ..."

"You used me. That was why the change of heart. Why you came to my room that night. Not that you liked me. You didn't want to date me at all until you saw me as being useful."

She shook her head furiously. "That's not true. I really like you. I just also knew that you could help me get into the frat. One has nothing to do with the other. All the stuff I told you about the bad break up and not being ready to date was true. I was ... I was attacked by my last boyfriend. I haven't dated anyone since. I didn't want to date anyone until I met you. You have to believe me."

"I'm not sure what to believe, Selena. What else did you lie to me about?"

"That's everything, I swear." Selena put her hand on his arm and looked him in the eyes. "I really like you."

He glanced down at her hand. "I don't know, Selena. I need to think about all of this." He shook her hand off his arm and stood.

Selena stared as he began walking out. *Walking out on her.* She didn't know how to make him stay. She didn't know how to make up for what she'd done.

He reached the door and stopped. "You know, I really liked you, Selena. I would've never thought you were using me."

Liked. Past tense. She hurried over to him. "I'm so sorry. Maybe we can start over?"

"I need some time to think about this."

Her heart fell to the floor. "Okay."

He opened the door and walked out.

Selena stood in the doorway and watched him walk down the hall to his room. She supposed it could've been worse. He could've physically hurt her. *Wow, way to set the bar high. I guess this is one way to test someone to determine if they're an abuser.* There was no question he would've lashed out if he'd been a bad guy. He hadn't. Brendon was a good guy and she'd hurt him. She closed the door and slumped into the couch. *Way to go, Selena.*

19

Christmas morning, Selena and her stepsister, Zoey, sat on the floor in front of the brightly lit tree munching on sugar cookies as they retrieved gifts out of their stockings while Martina and her dad took photos of the two of them acting like little kids. She and Zoey compared the matching necklaces that Santa had given them. A gold cursive Z for Zoey and an S for Selena. The two young women turned around and sang, "Thank you, Santa!"

Her dad winked at the two of them.

Although Zoey, a sophomore at Oregon University studying computer science, was a year older than Selena, they had become fast friends when they'd met the year before. Both loved clothes, fashion, and makeup. Selena loved having a sister to hang out with when they were both home from school in addition to her best friend from high school, Alida.

There was a knock on their front door. Martina said, "I'll get it."

Selena paid no mind as she and Zoey set down their now-empty stockings and decided to sing and dance along to "Jingle Bell Rock" in their matching Christmas pajamas. They laughed and sang. By the last chorus they had fallen down on the couch, doubled over in laughter.

Martina called out, "Selena, you have a visitor." Selena turned to look up and her mouth dropped open. She hurried off the couch and smoothed out her pajama set, which was decorated with cheerful snowmen. "Uh. Hi, Brendon."

He shifted awkwardly in the doorway of the living room. "Hi. Can we talk?"

Martina turned to Brendon and gave him a friendly smile. "You can use the dining room."

Selena had no idea Brendon was coming over. They hadn't spoken since that Friday morning before break. She had feared that he had completely lost interest in her and never wanted to speak to her again. She texted him twice, but then gave up. She hadn't blamed him. Now he was here in her house and she was wearing snowman pajamas and no makeup. *Eek.* Thank god she was wearing a bra.

He sat across from her in the dining room. "I like your pajamas."

Was he flirting? "Thanks. Um, what are you doing here?"

"I wanted to wish you a Merry Christmas and I wanted to tell you that I thought about what you told me. I now see that everything you did was for a good cause. I was hurt and I was angry when I found out that you used me." Selena tried to protest, but he stopped her. "Let me finish, please. And I thought about what you said about maybe starting over. Not from scratch, but with a clean slate. I would like to try to do that. What do you think?"

Selena nodded with a smile. "I would like that." Christmas was definitely now her favorite holiday. She used to dread it before, due to the depressing nature and lack of cheer. But between last year, when she'd been reunited with her dad, and this one, it was the best time of the year, for sure.

Brendon's smile faded. "Oh, I almost forgot to tell you. Tyler called me looking for a roommate. Apparently, they're shutting down the frat because of all the allegations. And by the way, that friendship is officially over. I always knew he wasn't exactly a great guy, but I had no idea he was capable of such terrible things. I believe you and Dee. I'm not interested in associating with him or anyone like him, ever again."

She'd done it. The frat was shut down. She refrained from jumping up and down, instead she slid out of her chair and hurried over to him. She bent over and lightly kissed him on the lips. "Merry Christmas."

He beamed up at her. "Merry Christmas."

From behind, they heard a, "Everything okay in here?"

Selena turned around and met her dad's gaze. Even though she was almost nineteen years old, he was still the protective father.

"We're okay, Dad. Oh, and this is Brendon. Brendon this is my dad, Charlie."

Brendon scooted the chair back and stood up. He extended his hand. "Nice to meet you, sir."

Selena's dad grinned. "You can call me Charlie."

Martina and Zoey appeared in the entry to the dining room. *So much for romance.*

Martina said, "We are about to have brunch. Brendon, we'd love for you join us."

She put her hand on Brendon's shoulder. "Please stay. You drove all the way here."

Brendon nodded. "I'd like that. Thank you."

Selena said, "Great, I'm going to change out of my pajamas, and give a quick call to Dee to tell her the good news that the frat is shut down, and then I'll be right back."

Brendon eyed Charlie and Martina. "Is there anything I can help with?"

"Sure, come with me." Martina waved her hand toward him as she headed back to the kitchen.

Selena smiled before she turned and ran to her bedroom to change into actual clothes, brush her hair, put on some lip gloss, and share the goods news with Dee. Another great Christmas and a major victory, even though she hadn't succeeded in taking down Tyler or Detective Grayson. She may not be able to take all the predators off the street, but she'd taken off a few. That meant a few less victims and that would have to be enough, at least for today.

A NOTE FROM H.K. CHRISTIE

Yes, I know, another super light book by H.K. Christie! Ha. Not so much. Although, I do hope you found it enjoyable. My hope was to entertain as well as raise awareness. Violence against women is something that has been tolerated, overlooked, downplayed and frankly, been happening for *far too long*. It is horrific how frequent it occurs.

Early readers asked me about some of the statistics mentioned in the book and I thought maybe other readers may be wondering the same thing. The short answer is yes all of them are accurate (at least according to my internet sources). The long answer:

Yes. One in five women will be a victim of sexual assault in their lifetime. Other sources say it is closer to one in four, due to the fact many woman don't report their assault for many of the reasons discussed in the book.

Yes. It's true that the highest number of sexual assaults occur on college campuses between the months of August and November.

Also, yes. If you spray pepper spray in the mouth of an attacker it will have a greater possibility for incapacitating them

(Note, I haven't personally tried this, but it was a tip given to me by a police officer I interviewed).

During my research, I also found a tremendous amount of organizations providing support for victims of sexual assault and violence ranging from counseling to legal help to survivor stories.

If you have been assaulted or would like to learn more, you can visit rainn.org today and receive a wide range of information and support.

If you have been assaulted, please know, you are *not* alone. It was *not* your fault and *no* it doesn't matter what you were wearing or where you were or if you were consuming alcohol or recreational drugs. *If you didn't consent, it was assault.*

THANK YOU!

Thank you for reading *One In Five*! I hope you enjoyed reading it as much as I loved writing it. If you did, I would greatly appreciate if you could post a short review.

Reviews are crucial for any author and can make a huge difference in visibility of current and future works. Reviews allow us to continue doing what we love, *writing stories*. Not to mention, I would be forever grateful!

To leave a review, go to the Amazon or other webpage for *One In Five* and scroll down to the bottom of the page to the review section. It will read, "Share your thoughts with other customers," with a button below that reads, "Write a customer review." Click the "Write a customer review" button and write away!

Thank you!

ALSO BY H.K. CHRISTIE

The Selena Bailey Novella Series

Not Like Her, Book 1 is the first novella in the suspenseful Selena Bailey Novella series. If you like thrilling twists, dark tension, and smart and driven women, then you'll love this series.

One In Five, Book 2

On The Rise, Book 3

The Unbreakable Series

The Unbreakable Series is a heart-warming women's fiction series, inspired by true events. If you like journeys of self-discovery, wounded heroines, and laugh-or-cry moments, you'll love the Unbreakable series.

We Can't Be Broken, Book 0

Where I'm Supposed To Be, Book 1

Change of Plans, Book 2

JOIN H.K. CHRISTIE'S READER CLUB

Join my reader club to be the first to hear about upcoming novels, new releases, giveaways, promotions, and more!

It's completely free to sign up and you'll never be spammed by me, you can opt out easily at any time.

To sign up go to
www.authorhkchristie.com

ABOUT THE AUTHOR

H.K. Christie is the author of compelling stories featuring unbreakable women.

When not working on her latest novel, she can be found eating, drinking, hiking, or playing with her new 9 year old rescue pup, Mr. Buddy Founders.

She is a native and current resident of the San Francisco Bay Area and a two time graduate of Saint Mary's College of California.

authorhkchristie.com

ACKNOWLEDGMENTS

I'd like to thank my *Super Elite Level* beta readers: Juliann Brown & Jennifer Jarrett. Thank you for the continued encouragement, support, and invaluable feedback. Thank you!

I'd like to thank my other favorite beta readers & editors: Barbara Carson, Anne Kasaba, Kaitlyn Cornell, and Dawn Husted (editor). Your feedback was invaluable. Thank you!

I'd like to thank Emily Costanza for sharing her insight into being a college student and Criminal Justice major. Super helpful! Thank you!

A big thank you to Nicole Nugent for the copy edit.

I'd like to thank Suzana Stankovic who designed the cover. You did an amazing job with the cover - once again. Thank you!

A special thank you to my husband, Jon, for not only performing the proof read, but for his unrelenting support and belief in me and my career.

Made in the USA
Columbia, SC
26 February 2022

56872331R00076